MacMORGAN HAD BLOOD ON HIS KNUCKLES AND A WOMAN IN HEAT ON HIS HANDS

April Yarbrough had been all the woman that MacMorgan could want—but now Dusky was faced with a female who made April look like a schoolgirl.

Her name was Stella, and the moment Dusky had a good look at her love-machine of a body and felt the skill of her loving touch, he could guess how many men she had run through in her life.

MacMorgan had beaten four armed men to a pulp with his bare fists and the aid of a savage attack dog to protect Stella from ruthless violation. Now she was determined to pay him back—even if it killed him. . . .

EVERGLADES ASSAULT

SIGNET Bestsellers

EVERGLADES ASSAULT

Sixth in the MacMorgan Series

by
RANDY STRIKER

A SIGNET BOOK

NEW AMERICAN LIBRARY

TIMES MIRROR

PUBLISHER'S NOTE

This novel is a work of fiction. Names, characters, places, and incidents either are the product of the author's imagination or are used fictitiously, and any resemblance to actual persons, living or dead, events, or locales is entirely coincidental.

NAL BOOKS ARE AVAILABLE AT QUANTITY DISCOUNTS WHEN USED TO PROMOTE PRODUCTS OR SERVICES. FOR INFORMATION PLEASE WRITE TO PREMIUM MARKETING DIVISION, THE NEW AMERICAN LIBRARY, INC., 1633 BROADWAY, NEW YORK, NEW YORK 10019.

The first chapter of this book appeared in
ASSASSIN'S SHADOW, the fifth volume of this series.

SIGNET TRADEMARK REG. U.S. PAT. OFF. AND FOREIGN COUNTRIES
REGISTERED TRADEMARK—MARCA REGISTRADA
HECHO EN CHICAGO, U.S.A.

SIGNET, SIGNET CLASSICS, MENTOR, PLUME, MERIDIAN AND NAL BOOKS are published by The New American Library, Inc., 1633 Broadway, New York, New York 10019

First Printing, February, 1982

1 2 3 4 5 6 7 8 9

PRINTED IN THE UNITED STATES OF AMERICA

#《 I 》

Sometimes there's just no way of saying no.

Especially when the woman asking is a nineteen-year-old sea enchantress wearing one of those thin bikinis that swell and strain against a body that seems hellbent on escaping.

I had been enjoying a quiet July morning on my weather-scoured house built on stilts a mile out to sea where Calda Bank curves around the channel into Key West.

When you've lived in Florida for a long time, you come to treasure those summer mornings.

In the fresh heat of a new day, the sea is glass. Fish moving over the flats leave a wake, and you can hear the sound of barracuda crashing bait a long, long way off. The air is rarefied and washed by the rain of the previous evening, and the allotropic ozone fragrance of lightning is as strong as jasmine.

So when you treasure the morning, you get up early and try to enjoy every second.

Like most things in life, the morning is not the sort of

thing you enjoy by hot pursuit—like kids racing to open presents on Christmas morning.

It's the sort of thing you enjoy obliquely. It's the sort of thing you enjoy through the wayward eye, savoring and tasting like a voyeur. You have to sit back, pick out a few meaningless tasks, go to work, and let it settle upon you. The Zen people have a delicate image for such things. They use a snowflake. You have to let the flake settle at its own speed, follow its own course, because if you reach out to grab it it will just disappear.

So I was enjoying the morning.

I had awakened at first light, boiled coffee, urinated from the uppermost dock, then forced myself to do pull-ups and a fast half-mile swim before settling back for my attack on the new day.

On the Transoceanic radio, I dialed in the BBC at twenty-one hundred megahertz. The London Symphony was doing a piece on strings and timpani I had never heard before. It was controlled and fresh, and I turned up the volume so that I could hear it out on the porch.

Looking south, I could see the thin darkness of Fleming Key. Pelicans wheeled and crashed in the distance, and the eastern sea was a track of molten gold. I sat on the porch, back against the worn wood of the house, and went to work tying leaders.

When a half-dozen Bimini twists had finally gotten the sweat going, plopping down from my nose, I stood up and went inside.

I have to watch my beer intake.

In my line of work, an extra pound of fat can slow you a half step.

And a half step can mean the difference between living and dying.

But on a morning such as this, a cold Tuborg was a necessary indulgence.

As I said, you have to meet the good things halfway.

So I opened the beer, letting it sluice away the sleep phlegm and morning taste of coffee, then went back outside.

That's when I saw the boat.

One of those old flats skiffs built for stability and shoal water. At first I thought it might be one of the Key West bonefish guides. The skiff was typically overpowered, but the person at the wheel damn sure knew how to use that power.

The boat came arrowing across the morning sea in a perfect V-ing of turquoise wake. Had to be doing forty, minimum. The pilot paid no attention to the channel markers. Didn't have to. People who really know the backwaters off Key West can run the wheel tracks of crabbers or the intricate network of flat streams as easily as most people follow interstates.

And this person obviously knew the backwater.

I considered going down to my thirty-four-foot sportfisherman, *Sniper*, and breaking out the binoculars to get a better look at this skiff ace.

But I didn't have to.

The skiff banked prettily, followed the winding Bluefish Channel briefly, then powered off into shoal water my way. And in another minute I could see exactly who the skiff ace was.

She wore one of those dark-blue string bikinis that grab at the heart and contort the stomach muscles. And since I knew the woman, I also knew that she wore it more for comfort than for style.

A thousand years ago, she would have been the type to shake her head in disapproval at the figleaf breech clothes, and choose instead to run around happily and healthily nude.

For her the bikini was a compromise.

I went down to the dock to meet her after pulling on a pair of gray cotton gym shorts. She waved as she backed the skiff off plane, and brought her in starboard side to.

It was April Yarbrough, the daughter of a crusty old Key West friend of mine.

More than a year before, April had paid me the supreme compliment of falling into a girlish infatuation. She had flirted and winked and wagged that lush body of hers around, and finally I had to take off on my boat just to get the hell away.

Because the infatuation was mutual.

But in the meantime she had gone off to college in Gainesville. Her first month away, I had received a steady stream of letters at the marina at Garrison Bight where I run my charterboat and stay when business demands that I be in town.

But the letters gradually tapered off as her interests and her life were refocused—as I knew they inevitably would be.

You have to love the young ones from afar. You have to give them plenty of room to live and roam and seek, because if you make the unforgivable mistake of allowing them to give themselves too soon, they must ultimately end up feeling trapped.

And April Yarbrough was far too fine a woman for that.

So I had acknowledge the letters politely, and allowed them to disappear unchallenged.

And then buried my disappointment privately.

But I couldn't hide my delight in seeing her again. She really hadn't changed that much. The raven-black hair had been braided, and it hung like a rope down to her hips. There was the hint of Indian heritage in face and cheeks, and her strange golden eyes still suggested some ancient knowledge that went far beyond her nineteen years. Her body was lithe and long, sun-bronzed beneath the bikini, with heavy thrust of breasts and curve of thighs pouched beneath thin material.

"MacMorgan, you old fart!"

"April—you young fart!"

She gave the bowline a couple of quick wraps and jumped up onto the dock. Her excitement was contagious. I found myself lumbering across the dock to meet her halfway. She threw herself into my arms, and I held her closely, swung her around, feeling that fine body tremble beneath my arms. When I set her down, there was that awkward moment when two people share an uncontrolled emotional outburst without prior intimacy.

She brushed at her hair, gazed momentarily at her bare toes—then laughed it all away.

"Damn," she said, grinning at me. "Damn, it's good to see you."

"And good to see you too, lady. I enjoyed your letters—for as long as they lasted."

Her quick temper hadn't changed either. The golden eyes flared wide, and she put fists on hips. "For as long as they lasted! What in the world did you expect when every letter you wrote back was about as cold as old fish? I'd write you poetry, and you'd send back news briefs. Really, MacMorgan . . ."

I held up my hands, stopping her. "Take it easy, April. This is a reunion, remember." I held up the Tuborg. "I was just having a morning beer. Would you like a Coke or something?"

"Coke!"

"Or maybe a beer. . . ."

She yelled, "Coke! You still see me the way I was ten years ago, don't you, MacMorgan?" Grinning, she actually gave me a shove in the chest. "You still see me as that barefoot girl playing in the dirt down by Daddy's docks. I had a crush on you even back in those times, you know. I'd get behind a tree and watch you walk by. . . ."

"Does that mean you want a beer?"

"Yes!"

We stood toe to toe on the dock in the fresh morning heat. I noticed that she wore a delicate chain of Spanish gold around her neck—a memento of a treasure wreck her father, Hervey, and I had worked off the Marquesas. I looked down into her perfect face and felt an irresistible urge to kiss the face and never stop.

Instead, I held out my arms at the same moment she held out hers, and I hugged her warmly.

"Did I already say it was good to see you again, MacMorgan?"

"Just once. It bears repeating."

"Good to see you."

"And you."

"I saw that face of yours in one of those movie magazines last month. You were holding hands with some famous actress or something. She looked fat."

"Did you come out here to fight?"

She stepped back, her face suddenly serious. "No," she said. "I wish it was that easy."

I didn't like the look on her face. "What is it, April—it's not your family, is it? There's nothing wrong with Hervey?"

"Healthwise, you mean? Oh no, nothing like that. But he did send me out here. Figured I could fetch you into town as fast as anyone—that, plus I made him let me come. There's some of our folks up in the Everglades having trouble, Dusky. Bad trouble. And you know how our folks are. Trouble is a private matter. They aren't ones to go whining to the law. Daddy figures this particular kind of trouble is going to take someone big and mean and ugly to fix right."

"And he suggested me, huh?"

"Not exactly," she said. Her wink was the same as that of the little girl who had stood shyly behind the tree long ago. "I think it was me who brought up your name first. . . ."

《 II 》

So I walked her up the steps to the porch and then into my stilthouse. The place was built years ago, before refrigeration came to the Florida Keys.

In those back times, it was called a fishhouse—a stoutly constructed icebox built like a cabin to house a caretaker and the weekly catch of fish and lobster. One of the old-time fish companies would send a boat out to pick up the catch once a week—and bring more blocks of ice.

I had bought it from a sour old man who had had a hand in its construction.

He pretended he hated the place. He told me he was sick and tired of waking up alone every morning with only the wind birds and fish as neighbors.

He told me he was anxious to move to one of those retirement villages so common in Florida; one of those mechanized, prepackaged settlements that try desperately to turn the deathwatch into a recreation.

Sour as he was, I liked the old man. And I knew better than to believe that he really wanted to leave the little house built a mile out to sea.

A month after we had closed the deal, he returned for

the afternoon. He turned a dour eye on the "improvements" I had made: watercolor paintings on the wall by Wellington Ward and Gustave Ameier, a big brass double bed in the only sleeping room, brass oil lanterns for light, and a bookcase stacked with my small but good ship's library.

He had raved unconvincingly about the wonderful life he was living at Sunset Retirement Estates. Told me about the shuffleboard tournaments, the evening card parties and the afternoon arts-and-crafts classes.

I hoped the happiness I tried to show for him was a lie better disguised than his own.

Just before he left, he stopped before the ragged teeth of the bleached mako jaws he had allowed to remain hanging on the wall.

"Big goddam shark, that one was," he had said.

"Ten-, twelve-footer?"

"Twelve-footer my ass, young fella. Fifteen and a half by my measure—and I'm the one that kilt the sombitch! Started cruisin' aroun' my house here every mornin' a few years ago. Scared off all o' my snappers and groupers that fed by the pilin's. I'd watched them little fish so long that I'd kind a grown ta like 'em. Almost like pets." Then he had turned a blazing suspicious eye on me. "Suppose you've been catchin' and eatin' them little fellas, huh?"

"No. I like to watch them too. When I want fish to eat I go out in my boat. Sounds silly, but I know what you mean."

"Humph," he had said—but he couldn't disguise the relief he felt that I wasn't pilfering his old friends for food or sport. "Anyway," he continued, "that big bastard on the wall kept a-stealin' my little fish. Took me a week to finally figure out how ta get 'im. Got twenty foot o' junk cable down by the shrimp docks in Key West. Coupled that onto four hundred feet o' half-inch anchor line. Tied that onta my boat and baited with a thirty-pound amber-

jack. When he finally hit, the battle lasted all night. Fourteen hours I chased and fought that shark, him draggin' me all around under the stars. Sun was jest up when he finally turned white belly side. Came up gaspin'; that sweet urine smell of a shark about ta die. Funny, but after all that struggle and plannin', and him killin' my little fish, ya woulda expected me ta feel good about it all. But when you're connected to a livin' creature like that for so long—the two of us hung together by a rope all night long, both of us strugglin' like our lives depended on it . . . well, I didn't feel as good as you might think. I felt . . . I felt . . ."

He had made an empty motion with his hands, and said nothing more about it.

Two weeks later, I heard that the old man had died at Sunset Retirement Estates. It was a classic exit in a state geared toward vacations and old age: a heart attack during the last set of a shuffleboard game. The obituary made mention of his sole surviving heir: a mentally retarded son. It cleared up the final mystery—why he had sold me the stilthouse. Knowing he didn't have long to live, he wanted to provide money for the son. So he had parted with the only thing he owned.

I had my Key West CPA take care of the trust fund. A year or two before on a particularly nasty mission, I had become unexpectedly wealthy through a combination of good fortune and blind luck.

Money means little to me. It supplies the few material things I want—and that's all. I learned long ago that independence is available to rich and poor alike. You just have to have the nerve to grab it.

So I had the CPA make sure that the old man's son would have the best of everything for as long as he lived.

As the old man said, when you're connected to any living creature for any length of time, you feel.

Good or bad, you feel. . . .

So I walked the teenage beauty up to my stilthouse.

She surveyed my living quarters expectantly—and seemed disappointed that everything was nice and neat; clothes hung, dishes washed.

Anyone who's been on a boat for long soon learns that neatness is the first rule of good seamanship.

But women—even the independent ones, like this magnificent April Yarbrough—have trouble accepting the idea of a man's living alone in an orderly fashion without female assistance.

"Just finish your weekly cleaning, Dusky?"

"I clean on a daily basis. It's an old habit, April."

"Oh." She swayed over to the little library and went through the books. There is no describing that inexorable feeling of want when you watch a truly beautiful woman move: the rotation of hips beneath thin bikini bottoms; the sleek flattening of breast as she stretches to reach; the ripe convexing and curvature of soft flesh of hips and thighs and stomach.

"Did Hervey know you were going to wear that skimpy bathing suit out here to visit me?"

She turned holding a book and flashed me a vampish grin. "I'm nineteen now, MacMorgan. Off to college and a growed woman. Daddy has nothin' to say about what I wear."

"Then what would your boyfriend back at college say?"

It was a blind shot. I didn't know if she had a boyfriend or not. But in the moment I said it, I felt the slightest pinch of jealousy.

It surprised me.

"Boyfriend!" She actually looked a little guilty—and that's when I knew that I was right. "How did you know . . ."

As if suddenly aware that I had trapped her, she glared, considered throwing the book at me, then decided to grin instead. "Well, you're right. In a way. He's not a

11

boyfriend. He's a manfriend." She wrinkled her nose impishly. "He's a professor. He's even older than you. And," she added coyly, "he's got a lot more books."

"Great," I said. "Am I supposed to be impressed?"

"Why, Dusky!" She laughed. "I do believe you're jealous."

"Hah! That's a laugh. I'm just wondering what Hervey and your mother think about your dating a guy old enough to be your—"

"My father! And I always thought you were so broadminded. Now look at you, MacMorgan. Prudish as an old maid."

"You keep wagging around here in that bikini and I'll show you how prudish I am."

She put down the book, the grin gone. A new, softer light in her eyes had replaced it. "I'd like that," she said. "I'd like that very much."

"April, I thought you came out here to tell me about some problem your family was having up in the Everglades. . . ."

She came steadily toward me, as if she had just accepted my invitation to slow-dance. I found myself taking her in my arms, holding her tightly in a warm embrace; an embrace laced with more affection than passion.

And then her sun-colored face was turned toward mine; the high soft cheeks and full lips and golden eyes and raven hair, and I bowed gently to kiss her forehead. But she moved just enough so that I found her lips instead.

It was a delicate kiss; gentle, experimental. And then her lips dampened, and her body seemed to swell, and suddenly I was kissing her deeply; feeling her body pressing to the curve of mine; feeling the heat or her near-bare breasts and hips against my body.

"Oh, Dusky, I've wanted you to kiss me like this for such a long, long time. . . ."

12

"And I've wanted to. . . ."

The top of the bikini tied with a bow. The material came undone and fell away with a tug. Her breasts were wide and firm and coned; nipples taut and erect. She pressed them hard against my face, her hands tangling my blond hair in ecstasy.

"Please, Dusky, please . . . right here, right now . . . my first time. Please . . . oh, God . . . please. . . ."

So I lifted her and placed her gently on the floor; lips tracing the length of her body, some distant part of my brain wondering absently if it was right or wrong; if the two of us would regret it; wondering, always wondering—and always questioning the wisdom of the first encounter with that final intimacy.

But I didn't have time to question long.

She was trying feverishly to slide my shorts down over my legs. I was very much occupied with something else.

And that's when I heard, for the first time, the gas putter of a boat outside.

We had both been so involved that we didn't realize that we had a visitor until almost too late.

With an oath normally considered very unladylike, April jumped to her feet, grabbed the bikini top, and ran deerlike into my bedroom.

I stood and tried to adjust my gym shorts—and quickly realized that only a pair of heavy khakis would make me even close to presentable.

I grabbed a pair off the hook and slid them on, hopping one-legged toward the door.

I got them zipped up just as my old friend—and April's father—stuck his bearded face against the screen door.

"Hervey! I wasn't exactly expecting you."

He gave me a wry look. "So I gather, ya old lecher."

"Now wait a minute, Hervey . . ."

He came through the door chuckling, a big chew of

13

Red Man wide in his cheek. "You don't have to explain nothin' to me, Dusky. Naw, not a word about it. I'd rather have you courtin' that wild girl o' mine than some bookish boy-man up ta the state university."

He walked across the room still chuckling and plopped down in a chair. He looked at me and winked. "Knew that youngun come out here with romance on her mind, and I got ta wonderin' if she'd remember the business I sent her on."

"Daddy, are you followin' me? Because if you are, I'll be tempted to rap you on top the head with somethin' the size of a ball bat!"

April stood in the bedroom doorway, glowering. Her face was red and flushed with kissing, and her fists were doubled statuelike on her hips.

And there was something else, too—something that Hervey noticed the same time I did. In April's haste, she had put her bikini top on inside out, so that the label was easily seen.

Hervey looked at me, eyes wide, owlish. For a second, I thought he was going to swallow his chewing tobacco. Instead, he whoofed and howled in an explosion of laughter, slapping at his chest.

And then I found myself laughing, too; roaring at that endless human comedy in which we all, from time to time, play the clown.

April looked at us both as if we had gone stark raving mad.

"What in the world is wrong with you two men?"

I kept pointing at her, laughing helplessly. Finally, I managed to get the words out: "Your top . . . look at your top!"

She studied it momentarily, and then her eyes described wonderment, then shock. Refusing to be intimidated now, she sniffed with the air of royalty, actually stuck her tongue out at me, then sauntered back to the bedroom to correct her error.

We had finally gotten ourselves back under control by the time she returned. Hervey kept wiping at the water in his eyes.

"Are you men done making fools of yourselves now?" she said haughtily as she crossed the room and, without hesitation, sat down on the arm of my chair beside me.

"God," said Hervey, "she does have cheek. You got to give the woman that. Gets it from her mother's side, not mine."

"I don't know, Hervey—you've never lacked for brassiness. And I've known you for . . . how long?"

"Longer than I care to think about, Dusky. Makes me feel old." And then to April, he said, "Darling, I wasn't following you. You know me better than that. Just wanted to make sure Dusky understood the problem our folks got."

No longer mad, but still offended at her father's sudden intrusion, April gave the ceiling a queenly look and said, "Well, Daddy, if you think you can explain things better than me, just go on right ahead. But I've got better things to do than sit around while you men spit tobacco and drink beer and jabber."

She stood up airily, patted my hand quickly, and walked out the door, only to duck back in with that vampish expression. "And I'll talk to *you* later!"

"You can bet on it," I said.

Her raven hip-length hair swung behind her as she descended the steps and roared off in her little skiff.

"Got a will of iron, that girl," I said after she had left.

Hervey eyed me sagely. "I got a feeling you're going to be finding out just how strong-willed she is."

"You don't mind?"

"I'd be a fool not to expect a girl as healthy as that not

to like men. And I'd be a bigger fool to object to her wanting to see somebody I like and respect."

"I appreciate that, Hervey."

"Well, you may not appreciate it so much when I'm done asking you for this favor."

"So ask."

"It might take some time."

I motioned around the room. "Ever since I moved out here I've had an open calendar."

He nodded, working the Red Man in his cheek. He eyed the brass spittoon beside my chair, and I slid it across the floor to him. He expectorated expertly, and the cuspidor actually rang, just like in the cartoons.

"I've got some family that lives back in the Everglades."

"You've mentioned them."

"On my mama's side. That's the Indian side of the family. That's where April gets her looks. Four hundred years ago she'da been a damn Indian princess, the way she looks."

"Or an Indian chief—the way she acts."

He chuckled. "Ain't that the damn truth."

"I'm not complaining."

"Give it some time. We'll see."

He worked at the tobacco some more. Hervey Yarbrough is one of my closest, more trusted friends. He comes from sailing-captain stock, born and raised in Key West. He's squat and bulky, all muscle and thick black beard. The slightest movement of index finger triggers a flexing of cords in forearms that suggests a lifetime spent hauling lobster pots and shrimp nets. And what he doesn't know about the water and reefs around the Florida Keys isn't worth knowing.

But there's another side to Hervey, too. With the strength is an underlying sensitivity; one of those people who make the old saying about still waters seem very true

16

indeed. He doesn't say much, but when he's in the mood he can be sharp or funny as hell; one of those rare men with the talent for original insight.

So I gave him time to speak his piece. I knew how the story would come: the barest basics first followed by tangents and possibilities which might be suggestive.

I sat back in my chair and caught the foil package of Red Man when he tossed it, and we took turns shooting at the brass cuspidor as he talked.

Hervey said, "This family of mine in the Everglades—they're neither Seminole nor Miccosukee."

"I thought those were the only two tribes in Florida."

"That's what the books and everyone else will tell you. But it ain't quite true. You see, the Seminoles aren't but a combination of several different tribes that escaped into Florida in the seventeen and eighteen hundreds. Came here when the Yamassee were driven out of Carolina, and after the Creek wars and after Andrew Jackson drove the Cherokee out of their farms and schools and made them go west."

"Sounds like you've read up on it."

He shrugged. "Like I said, I'm Indian on my mama's side. If you want to find out who you are, you got to find out where you're from."

"So your mother's people are from Georgia and Carolina?"

He smiled. "No. We're Florida, through and through. When those other poor Indians came running rag-tag south, just trying to stay ahead of Jackson's dogs, there were still a few remnants of the Florida tribes around. Way, way back in the old times there were the Calusas and the Ais, the Tequesta and the Timucua and some others. Spaniards kilt most of them—not with their guns or their swords, but with disease. The books will tell you they're all extinct."

"But the books are wrong?"

17

Hervey switched his chew from side to side thoughtfully. He said, "Well, it's not something you could prove in court, but my mama's people have their ways and their legends and their word histories, and their word history says they're Tequesta. Probably the last living Tequesta on earth. Of course, they're not pureblood—not anymore. Couldn't be. Like my ma. She married my daddy, and her mama before her had some Spanish blood in her, so they say. All mixed up by now. But the thread is there. And they get real nasty when someone suggests they're Seminole. Not that there's anything wrong with that. It's just that they're Tequesta and proud of it. You've seen the shell mounds down here in the Keys and around Cape Sable and Flamingo? They built those mounds probably before Christ was born. They're the only true Floridans around."

"I can understand why they'd take some pride in that."

He chuckled. "They do. They damn sure do. Stubborn as hell, those folks. And it's probably hurt them in some ways."

"How so?"

"Well," he said, "the fact they refuse to connect themselves with the Seminole or Miccosukee cuts their political clout right down to zero. Back in 1957 the Florida Indians voted to incorporate under the Indian Reorganization Act. Strength in numbers, you know. But there was only my mama's folks and two other families who considered themselves Tequesta, and they wouldn't have a thing to do with it. What that means is, they're Indians on their Indian land, but they don't get one ounce of government backing."

"That's bad?"

"Hell no, not normally. But up there in the Everglades, there have been some things going on that *aren't* normal."

"What do you mean?"

"What I mean is, I got family up there tryin' to make a

18

living on two hundred acres of palmetto and cypress and swamp, and suddenly someone is trying to chase them out."

"But why?"

"Damn if I know. That's why I'm here talkin' to you. But one thing's for sure: Someone's tryin' to chase our folks out and steal their land. And we got to stop them. Stop them cold. . . ."

《 III 》

I recognized the look on the face of Hervey Yarbrough.

It wasn't a look I'd often seen—maybe only twice before.

Once was a dozen years or so ago when some rich New York yacht rookie started giving him a hard time over a bilge-pump impeller he had bought at Hervey's little marina. The goon from the Big Apple had stuck the impeller in ass backwards, and then had tried to blame Hervey for selling faulty hardware.

Hervey took his verbal abuse for all of twenty minutes before he got that look in his eyes: a sort of burning, squinty look. He had turned to the New Yorker and said in his calmest drawl, "You want your money back? You say one more word, call me one more name, and I'm going to give you your money back—stuffed right down your throat."

Fool that he was, the New Yorker proceeded to say several more words.

It was not a very pretty thing to watch. The New Yorker had probably never been in a fight that someone didn't rush to break up—if he had ever been in a fight before at all.

Hervey had gotten him down in the sand, hellbent on ramming a five-dollar bill down the guy's throat. The New Yorker kept craning his neck around, as if looking for someone to come and stop this madman. And every time he'd look up, Hervey would smack him flush on the ear. It didn't take long, and by the time it was over the New Yorker was spitting bits and pieces of five-dollar bill, and it looked as if he had a package of grapes attached to the side of his head.

So I knew that look. And I knew it meant trouble.

Hervey was the kind of guy who could take a lot of pushing. But once you pushed him across the line, there was no going back. It was either fight or die.

Someone in the Everglades had been pushing Hervey's family. And when it comes to the Yarbroughs—and a lot of other native Key Westers—if you've pushed one, you've pushed them all.

As April had told me earlier, they weren't the kind to go crying to the law. Instead, he had come to me for help.

And if there was ever anyone I owed a favor, it was Hervey Yarbrough. And his family. It seemed like a lifetime ago that I had taken my revenge on the drug pirates who had killed my family and best friend.

Afterward, it was Hervey's family who took me in, cared for me and hid me. So I owed him one. A big one.

"What makes you think someone is trying to push your mother's people off their land?" I asked.

He paused, throat dry from talking. A quiet man, he wasn't used to so much vocal strain. He rubbed at his neck meaningfully. "Don't suppose you have any cold beer out here, Dusky?"

I stood and went to the little gas refrigerator. I was down to a good weight, two-fifteen, and I had been swimming every day and doing my pull-ups. I was in good

21

shape, eating the right food, mind and body in fine shape, so I grabbed a beer for myself too.

"Tuborg okay?"

"Since you made me rich by finding that treasure, it's just about the only thing I drink. Fine beer."

"It is that."

I cracked open the two bottles of beer and handed him his. He took half of it in a swallow and wiped his mouth.

"Nothing like that first taste of beer," he said.

"Nothing like it."

So he told me about his Indian relatives who lived deep in the Everglades and about the problems they were having.

There had been three families in the area who considered themselves Tequesta. One of the families had gradually dissipated and then disappeared through marriage and old age.

That left Hervey's relatives and another family. The two of them acquired and divided the third family's land—not as easy as it sounded.

The fact that a small group of Indians lived in the Everglades who refused to be classified as Seminole or Miccosukee put the government in an awkward situation. Was the abandoned land private or public? Should it become part of the Big Cypress National Park Reservation system, or should it be divided among those remaining Indians who claimed to be Tequesta?

To avoid any public notice or news media uproar, the government people suggested to the two families that they just divide the land and not say another word about it. The government workers—typically fearful for their jobs or of undue notice—didn't want to set any unhappy precedents.

So the whole thing was done quietly. In fact, according to Hervey, only the two families and the people involved with Indian Affairs knew about it.

"So that gave them two hundred acres in the Everglades?"

Hervey nodded. "Give or take a few acres. The other family there has about the same. Not all that much when you consider the size of the Everglades, but it's beautiful land. Used to go there and stay in the summer when I was a boy. Cypress heads like you've never seen, and clear streams and bass as big as this. All sorts of gators and snakes and deer and bear. Great place for a boy. Almost turned me against living by the sea, it was such a fine place."

"I can't imagine you living away from the water."

He shrugged. "That's because you haven't spent much time in the Everglades. You can't see much from the Tamiami Trail or Alligator Alley. You got to get back in. Way in." He sighed, remembering, and he looked at the tin roof of my stilthouse as he spoke. "You walk through those pine and myrtle plains for a while, and it's hot and dry and sticky, and just thinking about it makes you thirsty. And then you see this cypress head in the distance, and it looks silver and dark and cool, like an island. And then you walk in through between the smallest hatrack cypress on their pyramid trunks and it's like entering a church. The big cypress bends over you like a cathedral, letting in just these long beams of sunlight, and there's a pond in the middle with white orchids growing on them silver trees, and there's moss draping down and air plants, and you can see gators in the pond like old logs, and the water is so clear you can see the bass moving before they strike. Deer go to water there, and there's turtles on the logs, and the big white egrets flap off through those beams of sunlight, and there's always that freshwater coolness there."

"It does sound nice."

"It is. My mama being Tequesta and all, I could have settled there by rights."

23

"But you didn't."

"No, I didn't. Sometimes when the tourists come driving down like maniacs to Key West with their campers and their mobile homes and their speedboats, talkin' loud and actin' like they own the place, I kind of regret it."

"Just sometimes?"

He smiled. "Just sometimes."

I finished my beer and got us two more.

"So who controls this land?" I asked. "State government or federal government?"

"Neither," he said. "That's the unusual thing about it. It's not reservation land, so the federal people have no say about it. It's Indian land, so the state doesn't have anything to do with it. You might say the Tequesta there are the only folks in all America who really own their own property."

"I can think of some reasons why someone might want to take it away."

"I can too," he said.

"So how are they trying to chase your folks off?"

He paused for a moment, suddenly unsure. "Well," he said finally, "whoever's doing it is going about it in a pretty strange way."

"How so?"

"It's just that they're not making it impossible to live there—just uncomfortable."

"If I'm going to help, Hervey, you've got to give me some specifics."

"I know, I know. It's just that it's going to sound kind of silly, some of the things."

"Most of my life, it seems like I've majored in Silly."

He grinned. "Don't we all?"

"Gets to be habit-forming, I guess."

"God knows." He wiped his face with a sun-scarred hand. "Okay," he said, "you asked for it: You ever hear of a creature called the Swamp Ape?"

I tried to swallow my involuntary smile. Coming from Hervey, a model of the pragmatic and conservative, it did indeed sound silly.

"You mean Florida's version of the Abominable Snowman?"

"You know damn well that's what I mean. And if you're gonna sit there laughin' at me, I ain't goin' to tell you about it."

"Sorry," I said quickly. "It's just that you sort of took me by surprise."

"Well, it took me by surprise, too. The folks I got living up there in the Everglades are my old granddaddy, an aunt that's young enough to be my daughter and her husband. Got some distant relatives moving in and out from time to time, but that's the heart of the family."

"And this Swamp Ape is trying to chase them off?"

"Dammit," he said, "do you want me to tell the story or don't you?"

"Go ahead," I said. "I've never seen you uncomfortable with a story before. It's a new side."

"*Humph*," he said. "Okay, these folks of mine aren't the superstitious type—except for Granddaddy, who kind of sticks to the old ways. That young aunt of mine has a college eduation, and she works with the Seminole kids on the reservation. Her husband works as a car mechanic when he's not drinking himself to death.

"Up there in the Everglades," he continued, "the legend of the Swamp Ape goes back a lot farther than them books about Big Foot you've seen around. My granddaddy told me about it when I was a boy, just like his granddaddy told *him*. Used to scare the hell out of me."

"I didn't know it was such an old legend."

"It is," he said. "From what my granddaddy says, it goes clear back to the beginning and then some. I forget the Indian name for the thing, but it means 'stink monster' or something like that."

25

"Those people who . . . believe in it sometimes call it 'Skunk Ape,' don't they?"

"The people who believe in it do," he said evenly—making it very clear that he didn't believe in it. "According to my granddaddy's legends, this Swamp Ape is more ghost than animal. No one can ever catch it, and you can't hurt it by shooting it. He told me all people and animals are on this earth for a purpose, and the purpose of the Swamp Ape was to guard the spirits of the dead."

"The Indian dead, you mean."

"That far back in the 'glades, what other kind of dead is there? That's why it used to scare me so when I was a boy. On my folks' property, way back in, there's a big burial mound. Made of pure sand. Not a shell or stick in it. I used to wonder how they could get such pure sand so far inland. After a bad storm you could go back to that mound and find bits of bone and pretty blue and gold chevron beads right on the surface, washed out by the rain."

"You used to hunt for that stuff?"

"Yeah, but not for long. My granddaddy caught me one morning. I thought he was going to lick the hide off me. Instead he told me that the mound was sacred, and that anybody who messed with it would end up in bad trouble. And that's when he told me about that swamp monster—the one who protects the dead."

"It seems to me that if there is such a creature, your grandfather, at least, would consider it to be on your family's side."

Hervey nodded. "Normally, I guess—yeah. But like I said, that granddaddy of mine is a very old man. Somewhere in his nineties by now. And my young aunt's husband is a no-account, and don't give a damn about the land. What I'm getting at, Dusky, is some of those low-life artifact hunters have been sneaking onto their property and robbing that mound. You know the blue-collar creeps from Fort Myers or Naples or Miami who sneak around on Indian property hunting for bones and pottery and beads to sell, or just so they can take them home and tell their friends that they're archaeology experts or something."

"Yeah," I said, "I know the type. I'd rather spend a week with the summer flu than one afternoon with one of those jerks."

He grinned. "I'm glad we feel the same way about it."

"We do."

"Well, those bastards have been robbing the mound. Talked to my young aunt a week ago, and then again yesterday when she finally asked me to come up and help. Seems that a few days after they found the first signs of the treasure hunters, they woke up one morning to find these giant footprints outside their door. My granddaddy said there was no doubt what had made them. Said the Swamp Ape was looking for the men who had robbed the mound. Two days later they went into Naples for supplies, and they come back to find their house ransacked. Damn place just torn apart. High up on one of the ceiling beams, they found a muddy print." Hervey paused dramatically, then added: "It was the print of a giant hand."

"Damn," I said, "you don't believe——"

"Wait a minute," he interrupted. "That's not all. Granddaddy figured the Swamp Ape was blaming them for not protecting the mound better. But my aunt, with her college education, figured it was just a prank by some of her schoolkids."

"What changed her mind?"

"Well," Hervey said, "my little aunt has this daughter, Eisa. Eisa's not but five or six years old. One day Eisa went out to play and she didn't come back for almost eight hours. My aunt was frantic. Couldn't get hold of her husband, and they have to go five miles to the nearest phone. Said she damn near went crazy with worry. But then that little Eisa just suddenly reappeared. Poor little thing didn't want to talk about it at first. But then she began having nightmares and Myrtle got the story out of her."

"She wasn't just off playing?"

Hervey shook his head solemnly. "Not hardly. Eisa told my aunt she had made a new friend. She said the new friend walked her clear across the Everglades. She said the friend was tall as a tree and covered with hair. She said her new friend never said the first word—just carried her off. My granddaddy says it's the way of the legend. The Swamp Ape never speaks. . . ."

《 IV 》

In the silence which followed, I watched my friend closely, trying to decipher exactly how he felt about the story he had just told me.

But his face gave away nothing. His was a broad, sun-blackened face matted with beard. Unlike April, who looked much like an Indian, only Hervey's stoicism suggested his heritage.

"Hervey, you don't really believe that, do you? You don't really think some half-man, half-animal carried your niece off?"

He snorted. "Do I look like one of those UFO-loving loony tunes to you? Hell no, I don't believe it. If I did, I'd just recommend my folks get the hell out of there while the gettin's good. What I believe is, someone wants them off that property pretty bad—bad enough to play some pretty crazy games. They kidnap my niece for an afternoon. What does that prove? It proves that if they can take her for eight hours, they can take her for eight days. And if they can take her for eight days, it's time enough to do anything they want with her. And that's pretty scary.

"But there's more than that going on," he continued. "Fire's a pretty normal thing in the Everglades during the winter months. Especially since the developers around the 'glades started digging their canals so they could sell their puny little lots as waterfront property to the tourist folk. They've been draining the Everglades to death for eighty years, and they still don't know no better. But by May the rains start putting the fires out, and by September, which it is now, the place is soaking and there should be no fires at all. But there's been all sorts of fires around my folks' place. Not natural fires, either. Someone's been setting them."

"No swamp monster would do that, obviously."

"Right."

"Did you tell your aunt that?"

"I did. She wants to believe it, but she's so mixed up and scared now that she don't know what to think. My granddaddy refuses to believe anything else, of course—or so she says. He won't talk on the phone."

"And what does your aunt's husband think?"

"I only met him once, but he's not the type to do much thinking at all—not without a bottle of whiskey in his hand, anyway."

"So what do you think we ought to do?"

Hervey smiled. "Does that mean you'll help?"

"You know I'll help. Besides, you're too old and slow to be much good on your own."

He chuckled at my kidding and showed histrionic fierceness.

"How'd you like this slow old man to waltz you around the room a few times?"

"No thanks," I said quickly.

And I meant it. Even well into his forties, Hervey Yarbrough would be one bad man in a fight.

"What I think we ought to do is go on up to the Everglades and sniff around some. If nothing else, it will give my aunt some comfort."

"They won't mind me, an outsider, coming in?"

"Not if you're with me they won't."

"You have any ideas who might be doing it—trying to chase them out?"

Hervey shrugged. "Normally, you'd have to suspect the neighbors first."

"You say that like you don't suspect your relatives' neighbors at all."

He thought for a moment. "I don't, really. The Johnny Egret clan is the other Tequesta family. I don't remember much about them, but I know my mama's folks and them have always been pretty close. Same tribe and all, it's almost like one big family."

"How many people in the Egret clan?"

"I don't know," he said. "We can check into that when we get up there."

"So who do you think is doing it?"

"For now, your guess is as good as mine."

I thought for a moment. "The fact that they live on property controlled, apparently, by neither regular state or federal authorities opens up all kinds of possibilities. Plus, you have one or more people who are clandestinely robbing the burial mound. Maybe they're looking for something specific. And maybe they can't complete a thorough search with your folks there."

"That's a possibility. So we start with the grave robbers?"

"That's what I would do."

"The idea of some creep dressed up in a gorilla suit stealing that little girl really pisses me off."

"I know what you mean."

"And if I for sure found the guy, I'd have a real desire

31

to fix it so he spent the rest of his natural life walking on his knuckles."

"Revenge and justice aren't always synonymous—but they sometimes should be."

He smiled. "I have a feelin' I've got the right guy for the job, MacMorgan."

"Anything for a friend," I said.

When Hervey had left, his little flats skiff disappearing into the pale horizon of sea, I slid out of shorts and khaki pants and resumed my position on the porch.

I had missed the morning. By my Rolex watch it was just after noon.

But that's the good thing about living alone upon the sea. It instills you with a sense of the infinite; a perception that makes a mockery of all watches and all clocks and all time everywhere.

If I had missed this lone morning, there would be a million more to replace it.

The morning never dies. Not on the sea, it doesn't.

Only people do.

The two beers I had drunk with Hervey had been just enough to make me feel useless and sleepy and lazy. A droning deer fly circled about my feet, and I gave him every opportunity to escape before catching him with a sweep of my hand.

High against the sky, a frigate bird added dark dimension to the gathering cumulus clouds, all portents of storm.

Far out on the flats, something caught my attention: a milky stream amid the clear water. To a fisherman in the Florida Keys, that is always suggestive. And unfailingly attractive.

I went back inside and grabbed the new Quick ultralight reel loaded with six-pound Sigma line on the fine

Boron rod. I gathered a handful of jigs, a spool of mono leader, and my Polaroid glasses.

My little Boston Whaler flew me over the clear waters as if on air. Pods of brain coral and turtle grass disappeared in my wake. Before me, a big ray materialized from the bottom and exploded toward sanctuary. A cormorant banked abeam the skiff, flapping, it seemed, in a hopeless parody of flight. I read the movement of water over the flats and brought the skiff well uptide, then shut it off.

The bonefish were feeding in a school over the bottom, sending up the gray wake.

It was a small school—maybe a dozen or so fish.

But very big bonefish indeed. From a distance, they were ghostly in the aquamarine shallows, their tails broaching as they nosed down to forage for small crabs and shrimp. Beyond, the sea blended into pale sky, blue and swollen and filled with promise.

On my third cast I felt the sudden weight which suggested a snag, but the set brought the snag alive and the reel shrieked like an alarm as the bonefish stripped off a hundred yards of orange line on its first run—a staggering lesson in purpose and velocity, all hellbent on deliverance.

I turned him as best I could, gained a full twenty yards of line, then clung to the light Boron rod helpless as the bonefish made another sizzling run in the opposite direction.

When the fish began to tire, well hooked, and I knew that it was just a matter of time and leader strength, I found my mind scanning the events of the morning, free to wander in that margin of delight where no moment could possibly be wasted.

I thought about April Yarbrough and that perfect teenage body, and about the way her eyes looked the first time I kissed her.

Every first kiss is filled with promise. But it can also be filled with dread. What right did I have to interrupt her youth with my wanting; my scarred-up past and future?

That's right, MacMorgan—take this nineteen-year-old girl and mold her into your own likeness. Pretend you are giving her your all when, in truth, you're just taking, taking, taking because you know no woman can ever replace the one you lost. Not even this girl. So admit it. At least to yourself: You have absolutely nothing to give. And even if you play the game carefully, you will only end up robbing her of that precious thing—her own youth.

But sometimes I'm a little too pious for my own good, and I felt myself grin in spite of myself.

She wanted some time together.

And so did I.

So why not let the chips fall where they might?

I could see the bonefish wavering in the clear distance, making a broad circle around my skiff. It kept nosing onto the coral bottom trying to free itself of the little jig.

Now was the time I should have gotten its head up and gone to work getting it in.

Instead, I let the fish take its course, giving it every chance to cut free. Even if it did, I had won as much from it as I could want—the pleasure of its strength, the lesson of its purity.

Besides, if it did break free, the hook would corrode from its jaw within a day, and it would be fine.

My wandering section of brain left the subject of April Yarbrough and drifted to the problem her father had presented me.

Swamp monsters?

Indians?

Grave robbers?

None could be counted among my few specialties. I was the anti-pirate; the sea sniper.

I had done all my work on the water or in the water. What in the hell did I have to offer the land?

Besides, how serious could it be? Somewhere in south Florida some artifact hunter had a gorilla suit hidden in his closet—and a plan to do something on the land inhabited by the relatives of one Hervey Yarbrough.

I almost felt sorry for the poor bastard.

He had no idea what awaited him.

He had no idea he was dealing with people other than the common mass of men who run and hide when danger or the unknown confronts them.

Hervey Yarbrough wasn't the type to run. And he sure as hell wasn't the type to hide.

The artifact hunter didn't know it, but he was playing kids' games with a guy who wanted to see him spend the rest of his life walking on his knuckles.

I chuckled to myself. If anybody could see to that, Hervey could.

And if he needed help, I'd be right there beside him.

When the bonefish had given its all, I brought him to the side of the boat without a net. It was a nice fish, well over twelve pounds.

I held him carefully behind the head, taking care not to squeeze or touch his gill network. I removed the hook with my left hand, then cruised him back and forth through the water, reviving him.

The old man had been right about the fish that fight well. When you are connected with them for a time on line or rope, you begin to feel both compassion and kinship.

When I was sure that he was well, I released him.

He was suspicious of his new freedom at first.

But finally, he arrowed away from me through the clear water over the bottom, silver and lovely and pure once again. . . .

* * *

The next morning, I waited while the glow plugs warmed, then started my thirty-four-foot charterboat, *Sniper*, and cruised down Calda Channel toward Key West.

It was one of those molten September mornings with sea and sky looking blazed and blue and metallic.

I had spoken with Hervey the night before on the VHF. He had wanted to take his car north to the Everglades. Said it would be a hell of a lot faster and, besides, we'd have transportation once we got there.

And he was right. But I still vetoed the idea.

I have one big phobia. I've had more brushes with death than your average laboratory rat, but I still have this horror of car wrecks. They're such a damnably tragic waste.

Too many lunatic drivers on the highway who try to make up with their macho driving what they lack as men. The gearshift becomes an extension of their penis, and they think that close calls in the passing lane prove something.

All it proves is that they're as childish as they are stupid.

On those rare occasions when I do drive, I travel at the speed limit. Neither faster nor slower. On the average thirty-mile trip, you save yourself less than five minutes if you drive seventy miles per hour instead of the preferred fifty-five—usually a lot less, because that's on a straightaway.

I don't like to deal with the stupid men-children on those narrow asphalt stretches—especially the deadly A1A Highway that courses the Keys.

Their carelessness or their immaturity could cost me a day, or a week—or a lifetime.

I don't travel anyplace by car that I can go by water.

We all have our quirks, and those monoxide-scented carnage machines are one of mine.

I was surprised that April Yarbrough was waiting for me when I arrived at the docks at Garrison Bight.

She wore brief blue running shorts, sandals, and a white T-shirt that traced the curve and sudden heavy thrust of her. She had combed her raven hair out so that it hung like a shawl down to her hips.

She was smiling.

"Recover from yesterday morning?"

While I worked at the lines, I answered, "Not totally. But I'm afraid neither of us has much time for therapy today."

"Yeah," she said, almost pouting. "Daddy told me you two men are taking off for the 'glades this afternoon."

"Duty calls."

"Damn your duty."

"That's not a very democratic attitude."

"And what does democracy have to do with pure animal lust?"

I laughed with her, kissed her briefly as I stepped onto the dock, and took her hand. The early tourists, dressed in their Bermudas and gaudy shirts, roamed along charterboat row, and they watched us from the corner of their eyes. I could almost read their thoughts: *See that beautiful young girl with that big scarred-up man? Why, he's almost old enough to be her father! You can bet that sort of thing doesn't go on back in Davenport or Steubenville. What a weird place this Key West is. . . .*

What a weird place indeed.

I grinned and gave a half-wave to a middle-aged couple with cameras around their necks.

The woman actually lifted her nose and sniffed.

April saw it, and we laughed together. "Are we scandalous, Dusky?" she asked.

"In Key West, we're as conservative as a brown suit. Back in Iowa we'd probably be tarred and feathered and run out of town."

37

"Pshaw! You've never even been in the Buckeye State."

"Yes I have. And it's Hawkeye, not Buckeye. When I was a kid with the circus we'd spend a long week there every summer. In Davenport they'd stick us at the low end of town where the river had flooded. You could always tell the circus people—their legs would be coated with mud."

"Sounds nice."

"Lovely."

"And you aren't bitter a bit, are you?"

"A nice guy like me? I'm just proud to have associated with those corn-fed folks. If I ever meet the Pope, I'll know how I'm expected to act."

"Scrape and bow, huh?"

"Yeah, but light on the scraping."

I had wanted to tell Steve Wise, the dockmaster at my marina, that I was going to be away for a while and unavailable for charter. But Steve didn't look as if he wanted to be interrupted. Steve lives on a big gaudy houseboat at the docks—the inside of which looks like a floating strumpet parlor.

Steve's a little younger than I am—about thirty-two—and he's as well known around Key West for his enthusiastic bachelorhood as he is for his endless weekend parties.

With his windblown brown hair and movie-star looks, he seems to the pretty tourist ladies who come to the island to be the perfect adventure to cap their holiday.

And Steve is always happy to oblige. He has seen more women come and go (the pun is not accidental) than the average YWCA. They love him so because there is absolutely nothing predatory about him. He treats them like royalty, wines and dines them aboard his *Fred Astaire*, and shares a tearful goodbye with them when it is time to say farewell.

He makes no promises.

They want no promises made.

And they all live contentedly ever after.

You can always tell when Steve has had a particularly strenuous week with one of his tourist lady friends. He sits in the sun on the deck of his houseboat blinking like some weary loggerhead that has just made the Gulf Stream crossing alone. He sighs a lot and speaks of things profound.

But Steve wasn't working his way toward recovery now. He was working his way toward something very different indeed. Three of them sat on the upper deck of his houseboat, talking animatedly: Steve and a pair of mahogany-haired twins who appeared to have all the qualifications for carbon-copy Playmates of the Year.

Steve felt me grinning at him; he turned, waved two regal fingers, and grinned back.

"How are things with you, Steve?" I yelled across the water.

"Very interesting—that's how things are," he yelled back.

He grinned and waved again. I walked April around the harbor to the parking lot at the edge of Roosevelt Boulevard.

She had brought Hervey's old pickup truck. It was an ancient Chevy that had more wear than rust.

Chipped white paint on the door read:

Yarbrough Marina
Full Boat Service
Cow Key, Florida

April took her place behind the wheel, found something Latin and tinny on the Havana radio station, and shifted gears expertly as she drove us through the light September traffic of Key West.

"Did Daddy tell you that I'm going to the Everglades with you?" she said nonchalantly.

"No," I said. "And he never told you that, either."

She flared at me. "How can you be so sure, MacMorgan!"

"Because I know Hervey, that's how I can be so sure. You figure that if I say it's okay, he might go along with it."

"Ooo, you make me so mad sometimes."

"Why, because I know what you're thinking?"

"Yes!"

She took her eyes from the road momentarily, leaned over, and gave me a quick kiss on the cheek and ran her fingernails across my bare knee.

"Do you know what I'm thinking now?" she asked vampishly.

"I do. Because I'm thinking the same thing. But who will drive?"

"I know a nice shady spot by the water where they haven't built any condominiums yet."

I put my arm around her and kissed her on top of the head, smelling the shampoo fragrance. "One of the make-out spots from your high school days?"

"Darn right. I used to lure all the boys there."

"Really."

"A cast of thousands."

"I know."

"And just how do you know *that*, Mr. Dusky MacMorgan?"

"Because I read the bathroom walls when I go to the bars in Key West. 'For a mediocre time, call April Yarbrough'—everyone writes the same thing."

She slapped at me and gave me a scolding look. "Mediocre time! Why, I'm much better than that!"

"I wouldn't know."

The smile left her face, a new look of uncertainty in her eyes. Suddenly done with our bedroom flirtation, she said seriously, "No one knows, Dusky. Isn't that awful? I'm nineteen years old and about as experienced as a Swiss nun." She hesitated as she drove, then added, "That's why you kind of scare me."

"I scare you? Come on."

"No. You do."

"How?"

"How do you think? You've probably had all sorts of women."

"Right."

"Maybe dozens."

"Dozens?"

"Maybe thousands!"

I took her hand. "I think that would more than cover it."

"But can't you see why you scare me?" she said. "Let's say—let's just suppose—that you do lure me into your bed. I'll be awkward and clumsy. I won't have a clue about what to do."

"It's a technique that's always worked for me."

She smiled. "You're just trying to be nice."

"No," I said. "I'm not. I've never read any of those sex manuals, or those magazine forums. Makes it a little too clinical for my taste. People study those things as if they're trying to get ready for a major-league tryout or something. When it comes to love, you just sort of follow your nose."

She wrinkled her nose impishly. "Hum," she said. "That sounds nice."

I reached over and mussed her hair. "When your time comes, lady—whether it's with me or someone else—I have a feeling you'll do just fine."

"Just fine?"

41

"Just great, maybe."

"That's what I wanted to hear."

Even after helping me recover the treasure, the Yarbroughs had not changed their life-style.

They still lived in the old Florida plank house with the tin roof down by the sea. Ragged chickens scratched in the lawn, and their big Chesapeake Bay retriever, Gator, slept in the shade of a giant oak. In West Virginia, the rural folks have junked cars in their yard. In coastal Florida, it's junked boats. And the Yarbroughs had their share: old boats up on blocks; a big wooden Chris hauled out on ways for painting; chunks of engine parts and outboards rusting in the weeds.

The mahogany Chesapeake thumped its tail lazily when he saw the family truck.

But when he noticed me, his attitude changed. He jumped to his feet, roared a warning, then came trotting up stiff-legged, tail like a scythe. He punched me once in the leg with his nose, growled, then looked at April for orders. He had bright-yellow eyes, like a wolf.

"It's okay, dog. You remember Dusky."

The Chesapeake grudgingly admitted that he did, pulled away when I tried to scratch his ears, then sidled back and plopped down in the shade with a sigh.

"I think he's starting to like me," I said.

"Oh, he'll never really like you—until you become part of the family," April added cryptically.

Hervey was in the house. He looked up when the screen door slapped shut. He had his gear packed in a khaki sea bag. As always, he had a big chew of Red Man in his cheek. He seemed almost embarrassed when we saw what he was doing.

The cleaning oil and cloth were spread before him on the floor. He had the cleaning rod in his meaty right fist.

"You never know," he said in explanation. "Up there

42

in the 'glades, Dusky, things can get real rough real quick."

On his lap was an old sawed-off twelve-gauge.

There were two boxes of shells on the table beside him.

≪ V ≫

"Daddy, you don't really think you're going to have to use that, do you?" April looked half mad, half just plain scared.

"Dammit, girl—this ain't none of your concern. This is man business. You just go on along into the kitchen and fix us something to eat."

That was not the thing to say to someone like April. Now she was just mad.

"Man business! Daddy, there's no such thing as just plain 'man business' anymore! And if you want something to eat, fix it yourself!"

"They teach you how to be uppity there at the state university?"

"You're damn right!"

"You know I don't like you swearing."

"And I don't like you and Dusky going places where you might have to use a gun!"

They glared at each other for a minute, then both broke into laughter.

They were a match for each other: both stubborn and smart, with an underlying sensitivity.

Like father, like daughter.

"I'm taking this here shotgun," he said.

"And I'm not going to fix you anything to eat until you get back."

"It's a deal," he said. And they both laughed again.

I helped Hervey pack his gear into the pickup. None of us liking farewell scenes, Hervey's wife and April said goodbye to us at the door. April hugged her father, kissed him on the cheek—then surprised me with a kiss full on the lips.

When she did it, her face flushed with a heretofore unseen shyness, and she disappeared quickly into her room.

Hervey got behind the wheel of the pickup truck and pedaled it roaring to life. And just when we were about to pull out, he snapped his fingers.

"Damn, almost forgot something."

"Yeah?"

He looked at me. "What do you think about taking that big ugly dog of mine?"

"Hervey, you know I love dogs—but I'm not wild about the prospect of walking out on my own boat some night and getting attacked by that Chesapeake of yours."

"Oh hell, he's just mean around the house here. Friendly as a pup when you get him away."

"I'm not sure I believe that."

"Besides, he's a good tracker. He'll help us run down that Swamp Ape thing."

"Haven't you read the books? Dogs are supposed to be scared to death of Abominable Snowmen."

Hervey picked at something on his hand. "He ain't what you'd call a normal dog. Besides, you and me both know there's no such thing. I'm telling you, Dusky, that dog's a regular damn genius in the swamp. Remember? I found him in the swamp. He'd gone clear wild and was making his living eating small gators and God knows what else when I found him."

"Yeah, but we're going to be spending a lot of time on the boat."

"Hell, he's the best boat dog you ever saw! Just jumps overboard when he wants to crap, then swims to catch up when he's done."

"You expect him to swim and catch up—"

"Besides, it'll make my family up there in the 'glades feel better with him around. They got a couple of small cur dogs, but they just ain't up to snuff. Be nice to leave him with 'em when we have to go someplace."

"Okay, okay," I said. "I'm convinced."

"Fine," said Hervey. "I'll just go and get him."

"You don't have to."

"What?"

"Look in the mirror—or just turn around."

The big Chesapeake had already jumped into the back of the pickup. He sat on his haunches, his nose against the cab window. The yellow eyes glared at me—as if he knew which side of the discussion I had been on.

"Ready to go, Gate?" Hervey yelled out the window.

The dog plopped down on Hervey's duffel bag and went to sleep.

Florida Bay spread away from the oasis splotches of mangrove islands, vast and green and seemingly endless.

Florida Bay is a tricky pocket of water. On a spring low tide, there are thousands of acres of exposed grass flats, all rivered with a complex network of deeper troughs that would take a lifetime to know well.

It's easier to follow Northwest Channel out of Key West, then cut a rumline northeast for Ninemile Bank where you can pick up the intercoastal waterway for Flamingo.

So that's what we did.

I ran *Sniper* from the flybridge, fresh dip of Copenhagen between lip and gum, a cold ration of Tuborg in my hand.

For as much as I am on the sea, the love of heading for open water aboard a boat you trust has never left me.

Away from the cumulous buildup of a land mass, the sky opens clear and blue and flawless. The wind birds and the dolphin that run before the boat are your only company, and it somehow recharges your respect for them, knowing they live and hunt and reproduce upon the far reaches of water, where few men ever go.

With nothing else to do, Hervey got one of the light-tackle Penns out. He rigged up a trolling leader, added a big silver spoon, and trailed the artificial seventy yards behind us as we cruised.

The big lion of a dog slept comfortably at his feet.

"Fish on!" Hervey yelled after a quiet twenty minutes.

At the speed we were going, I knew it could only be one of a very few species: a king or cero mackerel, or a barracuda. Or maybe even some wild-eyed amberjack.

But it was a 'cuda—and a big one at that.

I cut the throttle back and took some time to enjoy watching Hervey play the fish.

People who only fish fresh water miss a lot. We have the jumping monsters—tarpon and billfish and snook—which come out of the water much like giant bass.

But there are also the greyhounding pelagic fish which make long skipping jumps beyond belief.

The big 'cuda made a veeing oblique run away from *Sniper*, then made a twenty-yard skip that had all the velocity of an arrow. Hervey tried to bring it up short, but the fish got the best of him and stripped off more line.

"Case of beer that he's more than four feet long!" Hervey yelled as he worked the fish.

"You're on," I yelled back—not altogether sure that he wasn't right.

It took a sweating, back-creaking twenty minutes for

him to get the barracuda alongside—and there was no doubt that it was well over four feet long. It gasped on its side looking for all the world like the blade of some ancient king's sword: the chrome bulk of it blotched with black, its yellow cat eyes blazing, and its mouth a slash of stiletto teeth.

"You want 'cuda for supper?" Hervey asked.

"I don't know. This far away from the reefs, he's probably okay, don't you think?"

It wasn't a matter of taste of which I was speaking. Barracuda is an excellent table fish. I was talking about the danger of eating a fish especially prone to ciguatera, a disease toxic to man. For many years it was commonly believed that fish like this great barracuda became poisonous because of their feeding habits around tropical reefs. The truth is, no one really knows why certain fish can cause the tingling numbness of lips and throat and, in severe cases, total paralysis. The old wives' tales will tell you that small barracuda are safe to eat—but that's not always true. Another story tells you to place a penny on the 'cuda's flesh overnight. If the penny turns green, the fish is poisonous. It's a very strange disease. In the Caymans, they eat only the barracuda from the south side of the island, where it is highly prized table fare. Supposedly, only the barracuda on the north side of the island are poisonous.

But like so many things about the sea, few "facts" are sure to be true.

"Guess we just ought to let him go, huh?" Hervey said.

"Sounds good to me."

But before he had a chance to snip the wire leader, the great fish gave an awesome slap of its tail and freed itself.

I hadn't noticed the dog. He had been watching the fish in the same way a cat eyes a bird.

And when the leader gave way, the big Chesapeake

didn't hesitate. He jumped full-bodied directly onto the fish. He gave a loud roar, then dove under after it.

But the 'cuda was way too fast for him. It disappeared torpedolike through the clear water.

The dog wasn't convinced. He dove again and again, eyes wide open, searching the bottom in water twelve feet deep.

He looked and swam with the grace of a mammoth otter.

"You're right, Hervey. That's no ordinary dog. He's shark bait disguised by a fur coat."

"I'd rather let him take the chance than rob him of the pleasure," Hervey answered sagely.

"You mean he actually catches fish?"

"He's pure hell on small sharks in the shallows. And every now and again I'll cut a fish loose, and he'll jump in and catch it again."

"I think that 'cuda might have taught him a lesson had he caught it."

"You never know. He's caught 'cuda before. Never one as big as that—but, like I said, you never know."

Finally convinced the fish was gone, the dog surfaced, blowing water through its nose. He barked once in frustration, scanned the horizon, then defecated with imperial concentration. He climbed back aboard on the dive platform, his yellow wolf eyes bloodshot with diving.

"Mind if we get underway?" I asked the dog.

He gave me a sour look, then collapsed by Hervey's feet.

"I think he's ready," Hervey said, chuckling.

"How nice," I said. "I'm honored."

I climbed back atop the flybridge and headed for Nine-mile Bank.

The water was so clear, you could see the shoals of Bamboo Banks long before they became a hazard.

49

In the turquoise distance, heat shimmered over the shallows, and the darkness of them looked like a gathering of gigantic creatures.

On the swollen expanse of sea and sky, I felt very small indeed aboard *Sniper*.

After a steady hour of running, I picked up the markers at Schooner Bank, and just off intercoastal marker 12 I saw the first thin landmass since we had left the Keys: Sandy Key and Carl Ross Key.

Someone in a yellow bonefisher casted toward an oyster bar nearby. The mangrove islands were like trimmed hedges.

"Just about there?" Hervey yelled up from below.

It was a rhetorical question. He probably knew as well as I that Flamingo wasn't far away. He had spent his boyhood exploring the offshore reefs and the shallows of Florida Bay.

But it was his way to let the man running the boat serve as the source of all knowledge.

"Not far," I answered.

Once safely away from the crescent expanse of banks, I brought *Sniper* around marker 4 below the white sweeping beach of Cape Sable and headed east.

There were more mangrove islands now. They looked frail and desolate on the open sea. Pelicans and frigate birds roosted on the islands, and there was the harsh guano smell as we cruised past Murray and Oyster keys and the distant silhouettes of Johnson and Dildo keys.

The little settlement of Flamingo at the very tip of Florida proper was, in early times, a fish ranch and charcoal center. The pioneers there made charcoal by cutting buttonwood, piling it in neat stacks, then burning it. The boats would come across Florida Bay from Key West with food and supplies, and return with a load of coal—or cane syrup, with which the Flamingo pioneers supplemented their income.

No one seems really sure how the place got its name. Some seem to think that the big pink flamingos used to come there in large numbers from Cuba, going strangely northward out of their natural range. Others think early settlers there just mistook the pink roseate spoonbills for flamingos.

As I said, no one really seems to know for sure.

But in 1893, the first post office established the name—even though the rare flamingos you will see there now are probably escapees from the racetracks in Miami.

I brought *Sniper* along through the dredged channel, raising the concrete buildings and palm trees before us.

The people of Flamingo once lived at the water's edge in wooden houses built on stilts. But that all ended when the national park system took the place over in 1947. Now Flamingo looks like vintage government national park issue: cement block motel, restaurant and marina, with American flags flying and plenty of khaki trash cans with plastic liners.

I brought *Sniper* up to the fueling docks and shut her down while Hervey worked the lines.

Because we had gotten a late start, the sun was closing toward dusk. There were a few tourist cars in the parking lot, and several small flats skiffs and charter boats were tethered to the fine government-quality docks. I looked for the boat of a friend of mine, and saw that it was there.

Hervey came ambling up. He wore faded jeans and a button-up shirt that made him look more like a cowboy than a sailor. "This place has sure changed since I was here as a boy," he said.

"I don't doubt that."

He shooed a covey of mosquitoes away from his face and smiled.

"Bugs are just as bad, though. They're the one thing no government on earth can chase away."

I looked off across the water toward Key West, where

the freaks and street merchants would be gathering at Mallory Square for the sunset.

"If we hustle, we can make it up to Whitewater Bay before dark," I said. "We can anchor there, or just keep on going toward Shark River. There'll be some tricky water, running at night, but once back into the Gulf, we could be off Chokoloskee in a few hours."

Hervey put his hands on his hips and stretched as if his back hurt. "With me handling the spotlight all night, right?"

"Right."

He grinned and spit an amber stream into the water. "You know, if we could cut straight through the 'glades here, my ma's place ain't but about twenty-five miles away. As it is, we got about eighty miles to go."

"Doesn't sound like you much care for the idea of running all night."

"And the look on your face tells me you ain't too crazy about it either."

"You're right. So let's get a room at the motel so we can grab a shower, have a drink and a hot supper at the restaurant, and head out early tomorrow."

"For an old married man like me, it'll seem like a vacation." He gave me a wink. "They tell me the waitresses here tend to be real pretty."

"And if one so much as smiled at you, you'd break a leg running away."

"Hah! I ain't that old!"

I let Hervey take care of the refueling while I tried to hunt up my old friend. Hervey was right. If—through some strange vehicular combination of canoe, swamp buggy, and airboat—we could head straight cross-country, our final destination was very close indeed.

There aren't many roads in south Florida, and only two good ones in the Everglades—and they both go east and west. So travel is not easy. Even in these times, it makes

52

the few rural settlements there even more remote—and more than occasionally lawless.

But however far apart they are, people who live in the Everglades are a community unto themselves. They know each other and take care of each other, and feel it almost a duty to pass on the bits and pieces of fact and gossip they have heard when they meet.

And that's why I wanted to find my Flamingo friend. If there was some shady business going on in the heart of the 'glades, he just might know about it.

I stopped at the little concrete office of the houseboat concession. Outside at the cement quay, the thirty-six-foot houseboats were lined, neat and gleaming. Tom Healy, who runs the concession, sat in his cramped office doing paperwork. He looked up when I came in, hesitated, then smiled in recognition.

"MacMorgan, you old pirate!"

"Why is it you keep all your boats in perfect condition, yet your office always looks like election day at a campaign manager's house?"

We shook hands, made small talk. On the wall of the office were charts and plaques and letters from the happy people who had rented his boats.

Finally, after we had talked awhile, I asked him about my friend.

"Is Grafton McKinney still around these parts?"

"Graff? Sure, sure—Graff will never leave. You know that. He was born here and I guess he's planning on dying here—if he's not too mean to die."

"I was kind of hoping to see him before we pulled out in the morning."

Tom Healy peered out the window toward the parking lot.

"I don't see his jeep out there. He may have gone into Homestead for something."

"Any way to find out if he'll be back tonight?"

"Oh, he'll be back tonight. He's never spent a night away for as long as I've been here—and that's a while." Tom eyed me for a moment. "You look like you have something on your mind, Dusky."

"Nothing important." And when I saw that he wasn't convinced, I added, "It has something to do with some people I know up in the 'glades. I figure only an old hermit like Grafton would know anything about it."

Tom Healy grinned. "For a minute there, I thought you were the bearer of bad news."

"When I have bad news, I always write. It saves wear and tear on the nerves."

He laughed. "Well, if anybody can tell you about the Everglades, Graff can. He knows everything there is to know—and probably some things he shouldn't. . . ."

≪ VI ≫

Hervey and I paid cash for our motel room. Even though I had no plans of sleeping there, I tested the beds, found them comfortable, then lounged back while Hervey sluiced the day away with a hot shower.

Completely out of character, he sang "No Business Like Show Business" in a cracking bass as he washed.

There was a cheap seascape painting on the wall, and I found it did not come even close to the beauty of the seascape out our motel-room window.

The sun dissipated into molten gold upon Florida Bay, and the mangrove islands nearby looked frail but steadfast upon their small base in the whirling order of things.

"Dusky," he yelled out suddenly, "I sure appreciate your coming up here with me."

"Just as long as that bear of yours doesn't bite me."

"You'd think you'd show some gratitude—him out there guarding your boat and all."

"I'm grateful. Very grateful. Even I am afraid to board."

After we had showered, we visited the little ground-floor bar. It was dark and cool inside away from the bugs and September heat. Some mid-fifties music was being piped in from speakers on the wall, and a dozen or so tourists types sat at the tables with their drinks, talking softly.

Hervey wore fresh jeans and shirt. With his hair slicked back and his Gulf Stream tan he looked like someone who had just washed and gone to town after fifteen hours on a John Deere tractor.

"I bet I ain't been in a bar in ten years," he said as we took a table.

"You haven't missed much," I said.

"Seems like a nice place, though. Doesn't seem to attract the rowdy types."

"I guess I'd agree with that."

I should know better by now. To look at me, you wouldn't think I was the superstitious type.

But I am. I admit it. It comes from spending a boyhood with circus people. Along with professional baseball players, they're the most superstitious people in the world.

I should have known that the moment I agreed that the bar seemed quiet and benign my luck would change and something—or someone—would prove me wrong.

And something did.

Our waitress was a pretty blonde who looked as if she might have been a cheerleader and president of her class fifteen years and a husband or two ago. She had the look of worn beauty: still striking at first glance, but then you noticed the lines forming at the eyes and forehead, and her ample breasts seemed to owe a great debt to Playtex.

She wore a clean white uniform, bra and panties visible beneath. She looked tired, and her smile suggested a certain vulnerability and the knowledge that life is sometimes not all it's cracked up to be. The plastic tag on her uniform said her name was Stella.

She wiped our table with a bar cloth, added napkins

and a basket of chips. Hervey ordered gin with tonic and a twist of lime. I ordered the draft beer.

So we sat in the comfortable coolness of the bar, made small talk, and watched Stella as she went to get our drinks. As my eyes adjusted, the blank faces at the tables near us became people. It's an old habit of mine—and maybe a bad habit. I see strangers, study their dress, their mannerisms, then try to pigeonhole them.

I don't like to be categorized, and I shouldn't do it to others. But I do.

At the nearest table were a man and woman—both somewhere in their fifties. There was a bookish air about the two of them, and their clothes looked as if they had been ordered from the L.L. Bean field catalogue. They drank white wine and didn't say much to each other. Yet there was an obvious affection there, like old friends content with their silence. I decided they were a modern rarity—a happily married couple who had probably come to Flamingo for the bird watching. The happy older couples fill me with a certain reassurance. Their contentment bespeaks order and reason. I decided they were the type I'd like to have charter my boat. When the man felt me studying them, he looked up briefly, nodded and smiled.

I smiled back.

At another table were three beefy business types who were working their way toward a deliberate drunk. Theirs seemed to be a harmless vacation: leave the wife and kids at home for a few days while they fished and drank and acted silly in the Everglades.

I watched and listened to them for a few minutes, and decided that they were all pretty good guys taking a well-deserved break.

The other table did not fare so well in the MacMorgan Rating Game.

There were four men at the long table. They all wore safari suits of various shades and design. The obvious patriarch of the group was a man in his late thirties who bragged long and loud about his big-game-fishing exploits in South America and the Bahamas. The other three men at the table listened anxiously, laughing at the right places, nodding enviously when the patriarch's story demanded it.

The man at the head of the table had black curly hair and a swarthy face. His massive hand clutched a whiskey tumbler, and his big shoulders and belly strained at the leisure suit. I decided he was probably the head of some corporation—real estate, probably—and these were his important drones, following him around on this fishing vacation to brown-nose and make points, and generally bask in the light of their browbeating boss.

The drunker the guy got, the louder he talked.

"I'm telling you boys, fishing isn't a sport. It's a war," he was saying. "Just like business—it's you against the fish. Get it? You against the *fish!*"

The three men laughed loudly.

Hervey and I exchanged looks and listened to him go on.

He said, "Course, you boys wouldn't know anything about fighting a really big fish. Those piddly little tarpon the guide got us into today weren't nothing compared to a big blue marlin or tuna. Nobody in this whole shithole knows what real fishing is really about. . . ."

He made a sweeping gesture with his arm that included everyone in the bar. For just a moment he caught my eyes—then quickly went on with his story, talking a little quieter now.

"Seems like a real nice guy," Hervey said, his sarcasm thick.

"Zane Grey in a leisure suit."

"Maybe we can get him to show us what real fishing is all about."

"You mean, invite him aboard my boat?"

"Right," said Hervey, his eyes twinkling. "Only you and me won't be there to meet him. Just that ugly old dog of mine."

We both laughed.

As Stella, the waitress, brought us our second round of drinks, a man I knew well came through the door of the small bar.

He wore baggy pants and a long-sleeved shirt buttoned at the collar. He was in his early sixties. Everything about him was long and lean, poor but proper. Dressed as he was, he looked like a country preacher looking for lost souls.

"Grafton!"

He squinted through the darkness, found me, then gave me a slow shy smile.

"Why, hullo there, Dusky."

I stood and took his hand. It was like shaking a leather bag of bones. I had met Graff McKinney years before when I was still a skiff guide, running that little boat seventy miles in a day searching for bonefish and permit and tarpon for my clients.

Even then, Graff had been running his squatty little cruiser out of Flamingo.

Occasionally we'd meet in that desolate expanse of Florida Bay midway between the Keys and Florida proper. It didn't take me long to realize that where you found Grafton's boat, the fish were not far away.

Still, I refused to follow him in those early lean days—not so much out of pride as out of courtesy. On the water, few things are ruder than following a fishing guide.

But one day, something happened to Graff's boat. That old clunker engine of his finally went *whoosh*. The fire wasn't bad at first—but it was spreading.

Luckily, I was close enough to see what was going on. I gathered his clients aboard my skiff, anchored, then swam over to help Graff fight the flames.

We saved the boat. And I had made a friend for life. After that, whenever Graff saw my skiff, he would unfailingly wave me over if he had found fish.

And I did the same for him.

So it was nice seeing this lean old man again; like a face from the past, it brought back some of the pleasant memories of my skiff guiding years.

"Tom Healy said you was around, Dusky." He grinned then. "Went to your new boat, but there's some kind of dragon creature aboard that said you weren't aboard—and I wasn't welcome. Figured the bar here was the next likely spot."

After I had made introductions, we all sat down again. Stella, the fading beauty, came over when she saw Graff and hugged him like a daughter.

"You keep threatening to come in here and dance with me, and now you've finally done it!"

Grafton chuckled, half embarrassed. "Miss Stella, I'm gonna have to leave the dancin' up to this blond fella here."

She actually blushed a little. For the first time, I noticed her eyes: a fine Nordic blue, as if they had been created by a watercolor artist. "Well, that's fine with me," she said, recovering. "Just so long as I get the next dance with you."

When she had brought Graff the coffee he had ordered, Hervey filled him in on his problem. Graff never said a word throughout the whole story—just nodded his head from time to time and made grunting noises.

After a long thoughtful silence, he said finally, "I think I know your ma's people."

Hervey looked surprised. "Yeah?"

"The Panther James clan? And the old man's just known as James?"

"Damn if you ain't right. They live so far back in the

'glades I didn't know there was another white man that knew 'em."

Grafton McKinney just nodded. He said, "Back in the twenties, I worked some long hot months building the Tamiami Trail with your granddaddy, Panther James. Fine man. Bunked with him and worked shoulder to shoulder with him for nigh onto a month before he spoke the first word to me. And that was under kind of unusual circumstances. Ol' Baron Collier had us building that road out of muck and swamp, from Naples to Miami, straight across the Everglades."

Grafton chuckled and continued, "Heck, there weren't nothin' out there but about a million snakes and gators, and so many skeeters you could swing a pint jar in front of your face and catch a quart of 'em. Only the 'glades Indians, like your granddaddy, didn't seem to mind. In the afternoon that swamp became a hellhole, but we just worked on and on, a couple of hundred of us followin' that floating dredge in the sun.

"Now, the way ol' Panther James started talking to me was this: I'd gone off in the bushes to take a crap. Always had to stomp around first—to chase the snakes away, don't you see. I'd hung my shovel in a tree and every now and again I'd reach up and hold it for balance. And I was just about done—reached up one last time, but instead of grabbing the shovel I caught holt of a big old cottonmouth moccasin by mistake. I'm here to tell you, son, I took off a-runnin', pants down and all. Your ol' granddaddy just thought that was funny as hell, he did. Damn near wet his pants laughin'. Then in perfect English, you know what he said to me? He said, 'Only a white man would try to wipe himself with a snake.' How about that! For a whole month I thought he was deaf and dumb—and then to learn there weren't nothin' wrong with him but a damn weird sense of humor."

"You became friends after that?"

Grafton McKinney sipped at his coffee thoughtfully. "I was closer than anybody else to him, but you still wouldn't call us friends. The Miccosukee Indians are a shy people, but I have plenty of friends among the Miccosukee. He was shyer yet—that's why I wasn't surprised when you said he thinks of himself as a Tequesta."

"He never told you that?"

"Never said a word about it."

"Dusky here says you know the 'glades as good as anybody around. You got anything to say about that swampmonster business?"

The older man shrugged. "Some of the old blanket Indians mention it every now and again. I don't personally put much store in it. I've spent most of my life in them swamps, and I never seen hide nor hair of it."

"So who do you think might be trying to chase the old man and his family off their property?"

"Damned if I know. This is the first I've heard about anything like that going on. But I can tell you this: The Indians in the 'glades are changing. And changing fast. Especially the Seminole. They're really starting to hit the tourist wagon. You ever been to that reservation up near Hollywood? The old Indians won't even hardly go there no more. Because it's Indian land, they can sell cigarettes tax-free there. Got big neon signs advertising 'em, and they got a fast-money bingo parlor up there that seats over a thousand people. There's even some talk that they want to get Las Vegas–style gambling houses built—anything to separate the tourists from their money. Like I said, they figure because it's Indian land the state don't have no control over what goes on there."

I said, "It doesn't sound like you approve, Grafton."

He snorted. "Approve? Why should I? The damn developers around the state are killing the Everglades fast enough as it is. Draining and dredging and building—all the time sayin' pretty as you please that they ain't hurtin' a thing. And anybody with a peabrain *knows* they are. I just hate to see the 'glades die any faster than it already is. God knows, I don't blame the Indians. They have every right to be bitter—and to make a buck any way they can. It's just that I want those swamps to last at least until my own grandbabies are growed. I'd like to see 'em last forever, but the way things are goin' I guess that's just bein' selfish. . . ."

《 VII 》

It was almost nine by the time Grafton left, and I knew we'd have to hurry if we wanted to order supper at the Flamingo Inn restaurant.

The four guys in the safari suits had been getting progressively drunker—and louder. And they had been giving Stella, the pretty, worn waitress, a hard time.

Hervey didn't seem to notice. He seemed caught up in what Grafton had told him about the inevitable death of the Everglades. I remembered the dreamy way he had described the cypress heads to me, and I could understand his concern.

Finally, I caught Stella's eye and called for our check. She seemed relieved to be pulled from the demands of the fish king and his brown-nose court.

She came over smiling, our check in her hand.

"So you fellas aren't going to stay and dance with me either, huh?" she said, laughing.

"I don't even dance with my wife," Hervey said quickly, as if she really meant it.

"I'll dance with you, Stella," I said. "But after we get some supper."

She rubbed at the back of her neck briefly, wearily. "To tell you the truth, I'll probably be asleep on my feet by that time."

"Tough night?"

She nodded toward the table with the four men. "Mostly, we just get nice people in here. Good folks who are just here to enjoy themselves. But every now and then we get jerks like that." She closed her eyes and shook her head. "God, how I pity their wives. Guys like that think women were put on this earth just to serve their every little whim."

"Don't let them upset you, Stella. They're not worth the energy."

She smiled a thin smile. "That's the truth. You know, when I was younger it seemed like I knew how to handle men like that. But it's getting so now they just wear and wear at you until you don't know how to act. I end up dropping things and tripping over my own feet. I guess they intimidate me."

"You want me to say something to them?"

She shook her head quickly. "Oh, heavens no. I don't like trouble. Besides—they're not worth the energy, remember?"

Those watercolor blue eyes of hers caught me again, and I found myself liking this woman. I wondered what culmination of events or personal disasters had brought her fifty miles deep in the Everglades, waiting tables.

You could read a life of turmoil in those blue eyes. I could see her at eighteen, beautiful and fresh and naive, hellbent on romance and the American dream.

But as happens for all too many modern women, her dream had somehow turned sour. And instead of sailing off into the sunset, her face said she had spent her share of time just floundering for purchase, struggling to keep her head above water.

You have to like the ones who end up weary and

alone, but still determined to survive. And this pretty woman was a survivor.

"So you're telling me there'll be no dance after we finish dinner?"

She smiled. "No dance. But maybe a cup of coffee?"

"You're on," I said.

The swarthy-faced boss-master grabbed her just as we were walking out the door.

"This is my last offer, blondie—fifty bucks for the night!" he said drunkenly. "And don't tell me you've never sold it for less than that."

And suddenly I realized just what "a tough night" in waitress talk implies.

They not only have to hustle tables and wash glasses and smile for tips when their backs ache and their feet hurt, but they also have to put up with the ass grabbers and bleary-eyed drunks who find that a bar is the only place their machismo routine will seem believable even to themselves.

Hervey was ahead of me, going out the door.

When I heard what the broad-shouldered, big-bellied jerk said, I stopped cold in my tracks and turned to look.

There was an expression of disdain on Stella's face, backdropped with fear.

When he offered her fifty bucks for the night, her lower lip trembled, more hurt than angry. It looked as if she had just about reached the end of her rope.

She made an attempt to ignore him and just walk away.

But he lurched at her drunkenly, trying to slap her on the fanny.

It wasn't a smart move.

His hand somehow got tangled in her apron. There was a loud ripping sound. Still entangled, Stelle's momentum pulled him over sideways in his chair.

I expected the other three men at the table to laugh.

But they didn't.

Instead, when their boss fell, their faces showed only submissive worry—like dogs who know their master is about to go on a rampage.

I had figured the guy as only loud and boresome—not fearsome. But his men were scared of him, sure as hell.

He had ripped Stella's dress at the pocket. There was a gaping hole there, showing just a swatch of her skin-colored panties. She still trembled between fear and anger. Like a little girl, it looked as if she was about to cry.

"Goddam bitch," the boss-master said, jumping to his feet.

"Don't touch me," Stella said softly, backing up. "Don't you dare touch me."

"Where do you get off treating me like that?" the guy roared. "I could buy and sell this place if I wanted—and you right along with it!"

I felt Hervey's hand on my shoulder. "There are four of them," he said.

"Yeah. Bad odds."

"Should be at least six."

"That would make it fair."

"Any way of getting them outside? I'd hate to have to pay for all this nice furniture."

"That guy can buy and sell the place. Didn't you hear? He's rich. We can send the bill to him."

Stella saw me coming back through the door, and she started to angle toward me, keeping a close eye on the swarthy-faced guy. He pursued her like a cat after a mouse.

When she was close enough, I took her hand and pulled her behind me.

It brought the guy up short. It was the first really close look I'd gotten of him. He was just over six feet tall and weighed maybe two-forty. He looked like an ex-pro lineman who, in a pinch, could summon all the speed and strength of bygone days—but only for about a minute or so.

He was easy to read. Like all bullies, he'd go for the kill quickly—maybe try to get me down on the ground and punch me into oblivion.

"This is none of your business, buster," he said darkly, still eyeing the waitress.

"I'm a Boy Scout," I said. "I make a living protecting ladies from fat jerks like you."

"You can't talk to me like that!"

"Gee, I thought I already had."

Behind him, his three men moved away from the table. They were all sizable enough. But they had that look about them—that pasty suburban look of too many drinks and too many cookouts and too, too little exercise.

Still, there were three of them.

"I think you ought to apologize to this nice lady," I said.

"And I think you ought to mind your own business, buddy boy."

"Maybe we ought to slip outside and discuss this in . . . a little more detail."

"The only place you're going to see me, buddy boy, is in court if you so much as touch me."

I stuck out my hand suddenly. "In that case, I think we ought to shake and make up."

I grabbed him when he tried to slap my hand away. It was reassuring when he tried to slap me: His hand came around in a big slow arc, as if on trolleys.

And I knew I wouldn't have any trouble with a guy that slow.

As his hand finished its arc, I grabbed him with one fist by the collar, swung him around, and jammed him through the walkway.

Anticipating my move, Hervey was holding the door open.

He went sprawling out onto the sidewalk on his face. Neon lights threw a ghostly illumination upon the parking lot. The boss-master got quickly to his feet and touched his nose.

It was bleeding.

Hervey was ready for the other three when they came through the door. And he didn't give them any time to get the upper hand. He cracked the first one flush on the chin with a right, then caught the second guy cold with a left that carried his full weight.

They both went down in a heap, groaning and holding their faces.

But the third one was smarter. He poked his head through the door, then ducked back when he saw Hervey waiting.

And then he reappeared, a knife in his hand.

It was not the sort of knife you would have expected a businessman to carry. It was one of those stiletto-shaped fighting knives small enough to belt undetected to your calf.

Before the boss-master almost crushed my spine to jelly, I remember thinking that the guy seemed unexpectedly adept with it. Maybe he had had some training in Nam.

He scythed the knife back and forth at Hervey's belly a few times, driving him away from his fallen comrades. Hervey had left his own fishing knife back aboard *Sniper*, and for that I was glad. Knife fights are a messy business. And even if you win, you usually end up pretty badly cut. And I didn't want that to happen to a friend like Hervey. He was better off unarmed.

It all happened in a matter of seconds. I was watching the guy with the knife. Then all of a sudden, I felt a tremendous impact and there was a blinding white light in my head.

The boss-master had hit me from behind, all 240-some pounds of him.

It knocked the wind out of me. And almost knocked me out completely.

I didn't have time to worry about Hervey now. The boss-master had me down on the ground, throwing punches at my face. His dark eyes were bugged out like a creature gone mad, and I could smell his sour cigar breath as he wheezed with effort.

He got a couple of glancing shots in before I finally got my wind back. There was a metallic taste of blood in my mouth. Strangely, then, I heard someone whistling: a loud, shrill two-fingered whistle.

With supreme effort, I grabbed the boss-master by his safari jacket and threw him off me. I got shakily to my feet. And when he saw me coming at him, blood on my face and blood in my eyes, a transformation came over him. He looked like one of those pro wrestling dramatists begging for mercy.

"Look," he was saying, "let's talk this over."

He stuck his palms out, trying to hold me away.

"Naw," I said. "Let's not."

"I'm going to have you arrested," he said. "I swear to God I'll have you arrested."

"You do that," I said.

I gave him a solid overhand right that collapsed his nose. Blood spewed as if pressurized. It sent him wheeling backward—and that's when the guy with the knife came to his aide.

The fallen boss-master looked up at him through the blood.

"Kill them," he said in a wild voice. "Kill both of 'em, goddammit!"

While the guy with the knife held us at bay, the other two men got slowly to their feet.

Each of them produced knives, too.

And that's when I knew that we had had it.

Behind us was the concrete wall of the bar and restaurant. And they had all the escape perimeters blocked.

The boss-master had recovered his confidence now. He took the knife from one of his men, and said to him, "Al—you go bring the car around. We're not going to stick around after I get done with buster boy here."

"Right, boss."

His face pasted with blood, and his eyes bugging, the swarthy-faced guy came at me with the knife. He said, "You think you're a funny guy, don't you, buster boy? Well, I'm going to give you and your friend big smiles. Great big smiles. Won't that be nice?"

I'd forgotten about the waitress. She had watched all of this grimly. But when the boss-master came at me with the knife, she ran across the sidewalk and started beating on him with her two small fists. He swung to knock her away and caught her on the chin with his elbow.

She collapsed with an *oomph*, holding her face.

"Any suggestions, Dusky?" Hervey said out of the corner of his mouth.

"Yeah—teach me how to fly real quick."

"Maybe we won't have to fly."

"Huh?"

And that's when I saw what he meant. The shrill whistle I had heard—it had been Hervey calling for his big Chesapeake, Gator.

The dog came bull-assing through the neon-lit night, yellow eyes glowing like a dragon, or some hound from hell. His growl was so deep that it sounded like something rumbling within the earth.

The dog was no diplomat. It didn't stop to consider who he should attack first—it just happened that the boss-master was closest.

He never saw what hit him. The dog came off all fours,

all slathering teeth and fury, and grabbed the guy neck-high. There was a sickening sound of flesh being stripped.

"Jesus Christ!" the boss-master screamed hoarsely, clutching his Adam's apple.

One of his men tried to pull the dog off him. He succeeded—but almost lost his hand in the process. That dog was hell on wheels. There was nothing cold or calculating in his attack—nothing like the way a police dog goes after someone. The Chesapeake acted like a lion reincarnated from the days of Christians in Rome.

"The car! Where in the hell is that car?"

As one of the men said it, a big blue Cadillac came screeching up to the sidewalk. With Gator still in a frenzy, the men didn't hesitate. They piled their fallen boss into the back seat and jumped in after him. There were gunshots as they pulled away, but the slugs smacked harmlessly into the wall behind us.

I didn't know if they were just bad shots—or if they were reluctant to add first-degree murder to their sales charts.

Hervey was testing the knuckles of his left hand gingerly. They were already starting to swell.

"You okay?" he asked.

"It'll be a day or so before I can whistle," I said, touching my swollen lip.

The Chesapeake watched the Cadillac disappear, sniffed at one of the knives they had left behind, then lifted his leg and pissed on it.

"Anyplace you want to take that dog of yours, it's okay with me," I said.

"He does kind of grow on you."

"I'm going to order the two biggest steaks they have at the restaurant. One for myself—and one for him."

"I think he'd like that—huh, Gator?"

The dog looked at him and sighed as if sorry the excitement was so quickly over. He made about three circles, then plopped down at Hervey's feet.

"My God, I think they were really going to kill you!" It was Stella. She had gotten back to her feet. Her blond hair was mussed, and there was a growing bruise on her chin. She was still shaking.

I went over and took her by the arm gently. "I think they were considering it."

"I just can't believe it. I'm going back inside and call the police."

"You do that. And then you can have some supper with us."

She looked at her wristwatch and shook her head wearily. "I still have another hour before I'm off duty." She locked her blue eyes in on mine. "But afterwards? I'd like to see you afterwards. Maybe we can have a drink. And calm down."

"Sure," I said.

She took out her order pad and scribbled something on the back.

"That's my apartment number. Stop by in an hour or so. I need a shower. Maybe that'll help. I'd like to wash this whole night away. . . ."

≪ VIII ≫

She was still in the shower when I got to her apartment. The room smelled of light perfume and soap, and there was a maidenly neatness about the place.

Earlier, before I left to see her, there had been an awkward moment with Hervey. After all, it had been pretty obvious that his daughter was interested in me—and that I was interested in her.

But he had just laughed it away. "My God," he had said, "go see the poor woman. After what happened to her, she's in no frame of mind to be alone."

So we had eaten our steaks and walked back to *Sniper* to present Gator his. He accepted the pound of raw meat from my hand as if it was expected—and just what in the hell took me so long?

"I probably won't be gone more than an hour," I told Hervey.

"For God's sake, MacMorgan, quite actin' like a guilty husband. You're a growed man. Stay as long as you like—or for as long as that lady needs you."

"I'm just trying to tell you what my plans are."

"And dammit, I'm just tryin' to tell you I don't care

what your plans are. I'm gonna have me another shower, carry a couple of cold beers up to that motel room, turn the air conditioner up full, and then watch Johnny Carson on TV. I got a feelin' we ain't gonna have much time for fun up in the 'glades."

"It hasn't exactly been a circus here."

"That's the damn truth!" He eyed his swollen hand ruefully, then chuckled. "But hell, it's been too long since I've been in a fight. Makes a guy feel young. I have half a mind to pay a visit to that pretty blond waitress myself."

"Sure you do," I said. "Sure."

I walked along the docks and across the parking lot through the warm September night. There was the fragrance of lime in the air. Mosquitoes whined in my ears, and far out in the darkness of Florida Bay was one frail light—the solitary light which marks the night strongholds of human existence in all rural or desolate places.

When I knocked on her apartment door, I heard Stella call, "Dusky?"

"Right."

"Give me just a sec, huh?"

I waited outside, swatting mosquitoes. Finally, the door cracked open. A pale eye acertained that it was me, then the door swung open completely, accompanied by a cold blast of air conditioning.

I hurried inside.

She told me she hadn't finished her shower. She had a big bath towel wrapped around her, and a smaller towel tied around her hair.

"Boy," she said awkwardly, "I'm glad you came."

And for lack of anything better to say, I answered, "Me too. Go on and finish your shower."

With her hair covered by the towel, the bare lines and structure of her face stood out. She had one of those ranch-woman faces: skin weathered and slightly lined, the childish blue eyes peering out tremulously and in mild surprise that she, too, was growing older.

And if her face didn't tell you that she had once been the vision of youth and beauty, the rest of her certainly did. She had long tapering legs wood-colored with sun, and her hips were so slim they suggested that, at one time or another in her life, she would probably have trouble with childbirth.

"You want a drink?"

"Beer's fine."

"I brought some of the Tuborg with me—isn't that the kind of beer you were drinking tonight?"

"That was thoughtful, Stella."

"It's in the icebox. If you don't mind, I'd like a gin and tonic. And call me Stell, okay? All my friends call me Stell."

Stell went back to her shower while I fumbled around in the little kitchen, making her drink.

If you want to really learn about someone, study the place where he or she lives. It can tell you more about what people are and who they are in five minutes then they can tell you in an hour.

So while I made the drink, I studied the apartment of this new woman, Stella.

She liked photographs better than paintings. It's the hallmark of the pragmatic type. At school, she had probably been better in math than art or English. On the wall was a black-and-white photograph of a pelican in flight. There was a snapshot quality to the photograph. It captured nothing of that normally awkward bird's grace in the air.

The living room was small and neat, with the typical apartment furniture: couch and two chairs stuffed with foam, made to look expensive and sell cheap—and disintegrate after a couple of years' wear. There were little plaster knickknacks on the shelves and tables; toadstools and elves and green frogs. On the coffee table was a stack of benign magazines—*Ladies' Home Journal* and *Apartment Life*—and the only books around were a couple of gothic-romance paperbacks.

There was a sterility about the place that bothered me. It was like walking into a model home—nothing homey or human about it. The barrenness of her apartment was in complete contradiction to the woman's eyes, which suggested her share of miles on that living road of hurt and joy and the day-to-day routine.

Ever the snoop, I listened at the bathroom door to make sure she was still busy, then glided into her bedroom.

It was not exactly a gentlemanly thing to do—but then I've never claimed to be a gentleman.

On the night table beside her bed was one of those little gilded picture frames you buy in the dimestore. On one side of the frame was a photograph of her in a cheerleader's uniform. There was a big blue C on the front of her sweater, and she wore a short blue pleated skirt. She was a very pretty sixteen.

I studied the face of the teenager she had been. She had had a lot more confidence in those days. The blue eyes were a combination of joy and expectation. On the other side of the frame was a reduced copy of her diploma. I was in the room of Stella Catharine Cross, who had graduated from Central High in the year of our Lord nineteen hundred and sixty-five.

So that put her in her mid-thirties. I wondered what had happened to Miss Cross between then and now; what had stolen the confidence from those lovely blue eyes and added lines and worry.

I didn't have a chance to pursue it much further. I heard the water switch off in the bathroom, and I hustled back to the living room, grabbed my beer, and took a seat.

She came out dressed in a long blue bathrobe that set off her eyes. Her hair was wet, and she rubbed it with a towel. There was a growing nervousness about her, underlined with shyness. She reminded me of some small creature who, after deciding to venture out into sunlight, is suddenly frightened and unsure.

"I must look awful," she said, trying to comb her hair with the towel.

"Not at all."

"I dropped the soap and when I bent down to get it, my hair got soaked—so I just decided to go ahead and wash it."

"I can smell the shampoo. It's nice."

She exhaled slightly, trying to relax, then found her drink.

"I hardly ever drink," she explained as she toyed with the wedge of lime I had cut. "I guess it's because I see so many drunks at work. But after tonight . . ." She rolled her eyes. "I feel like I could use one."

"What did the police say?"

"They said they'd try to catch the guys on the road from Flamingo to Homestead. They said if they didn't get them there it might take a while. They're going to send someone here tomorrow to get a report from you and your friend."

"We won't be here tomorrow."

"Oh," she said in a small voice.

She sat in one of the chairs. I sat on the couch. Her body language told me much. She kept her legs pressed together beneath the robe, and she unconsciously crossed her arms across her breasts, sipping at her drink.

I could almost read her mind. She was wondering why in the hell she had invited some big blond stranger to her room. She was lonely, but had she sunk to the need of one-night stands? Maybe. . . .

She worked more steadily at her drink now, hoping it

would relax her. We made small talk; superficial conversation about Florida and the weather and our jobs.

Stella Catharine Cross was much like her apartment. There was a surface blandness to her that implied a good bit. It told me that beneath the surface was probably a complex and lonely human being who camouflaged her vulnerability with things sterile and plain and undecipherable.

When she was ready, I got up and made her another gin and tonic. She took it carefully, and didn't bring it to her lips until I had taken my seat on the couch.

And then, suddenly, her eyes were bugging wide, and her face was bright red. She choked, gagged—then coughed an ice cube clear across the room.

She looked at me wide-eyed, terrified with embarrassment. For a moment I thought she was going to run and hide.

It was all so ridiculous—and so touching—that I found myself laughing.

Then roaring.

"God, I thought things like that only happened to me!" I said, still laughing.

"They do? They do?"

And then she actually started laughing herself. She suddenly seemed to feel better. She got to her feet to retrieve the ice cube, but when she bent down to pick it up, she clunked her forehead on the coffee table. And when she brought her hand up to touch her face, she knocked over a vase of sea oats.

And suddenly she was about to cry again. "My God," she said. "I'm so . . . so *awful*."

I stood and went to her. She eyed me fearfully for a moment, then allowed me to take her in my arms.

"You're not awful."

"Then why do I feel so awful!"

"Maybe it's because you're nervous. Maybe it's because you think I'm going to try to hustle you into bed."

"Well, aren't you?"

"No. It's nice just holding you like this."

"I want to tell you something. When I invited you here, I was hoping you would take me to bed. You seemed so nice, like the kind of person you know you can trust."

"So what happened?"

She put her face down on my shoulder, as if we were dancing. She exhaled wearily. "I don't know. I'm just such a mess lately. I came down here almost a year ago. I had had some . . . problems in my life. I came down here thinking that if I just got away everything would be all right."

"A bad divorce."

"Yes. But . . . but I don't want to talk about that."

I walked her across the carpet to the couch, then sat down beside her. She kept her face turned away, but she still clung tightly to me.

"You don't want to talk with someone you'll probably never see again, right?" I said.

"I don't know. I don't know what I want."

"As I told you, my reason for coming here wasn't to take you to bed."

She snorted. "Jesus, I don't blame you."

"Dammit, Stella, it's not because you aren't attractive. You're very attractive."

She rubbed her face against my shoulder. "Thank you. Thank you—even if you don't mean it." She was quiet for a time. I waited for her to speak, knowing she was deciding if a stranger could be trusted to share her burden. Finally she said, "I don't know what's happened to me. I'm thirty-four years old, but I feel like a scared little kid of eight. Can you understand that? It seems like every day I get smaller while the world just keeps on getting bigger and bigger. I'm scared all the time—but I don't why or of what. I look in the mirror and I see the wrinkles growing on my face, and I just feel so damn . . . *alone.*"

"If it makes you feel any better, everyone on earth feels like that from time to time. Presidents, waitresses, fishing guides—everyone."

She turned her face toward me, and I saw that she had begun to cry. "But Dusky, I feel like I'm going crazy. I feel like I'm losing . . . my *mind.*"

"Maybe you are."

"Thanks!"

"What I'm saying, Stella, is not to let it frighten you to the point where it does drive you crazy. When I'm scared of something, I've got a trick that always makes me feel a whole lot better."

"I bet."

"No, I mean it. I think carefully about the thing that is scaring me. And then, very honestly and very methodically, I decide what the very worst thing that can happen really is. I don't sugar-coat it; I don't lie to myself—but even so, the ultimate reality of the fear is never as bad as the fear itself."

"Sounds like great fun."

"It's not. But it works."

She was quiet for a long moment. And very still. Slowly, she turned her head to face me. There was a look of mild surprise in her blue eyes. "You know," she said, "you're right. It *does* work. Just for a moment, the briefest moment, I could *see* the very worst thing that could happen to me. It was real, and it wasn't very nice—but the moment it seemed real, it was no longer frightening." She smiled. "Are you sure you're just a fishing guide?"

"I'm sure—and sometimes I'm not even very good at that."

"Uh-huh."

"But my fee for advice remains the same. One cold beer. In advance."

She wiped at her eyes and stood up. "God," she said, "I must look a mess."

"And the other part of the fee is that you stop knocking yourself."

"Because I'm very attractive, right?"

"You can bank on it."

Subtly, her face was changing. The confusion was gone, replaced by a look that was unmistakable. It was the soft-eyed, arched-thigh bedroom look. Somehow, through a combination of the fight and my dimestore psychoanalysis, I had slipped through her guard. I had made my way past the sterile perimeter of this stranger, Stella Catharine Cross, and was being offered the intimacy of her body in the same way she had offered me her fears.

There were no words exchanged.

No words were necessary.

Between all men and all women there is an endless exchange of communication going on that is far more complex than our surface exchange of vowels and verbs and adjectives.

We are so accustomed to it that we are rarely even aware it is going on.

But it is.

We never meet the eye of a stranger without the minimum question-and-answer session: "I might be interested; I'm definitely *not* interested; maybe, if things were different . . ."

Those are the basic answers to the most basic of questions.

And now, this lady was saying yes; saying yes not in an obvious way, but in a way unmistakable nonetheless.

I watched her move to the kitchen to get my beer. I hadn't been lying—she was attractive. Very attractive. Her face held its share of pain and wear, and her breasts were no longer the gravity-free breasts of the cheerleader. But, strangely, that seemed to make her all the more desirable.

So why did I feel the urge to make my excuses and get the hell out of there?

Maybe it was because I was thinking of the lovely April Yarbrough; or maybe it was because I don't subscribe to the convenient *Playboy* philosophy that all sex is good sex—however desperate, however brief, however empty.

Maybe hell. It was neither of those things, and I knew it.

This lady, Stella Catharine Cross, was one of the injured ones; one of life's cripples, and sitting there waiting to sweep her off her feet and into bed made me feel just a tad too much like a cat waiting for the fledglings to try their wings.

And thinking *that* made me feel like the pompous, pious son of a bitch that I occasionally am.

I did have the urge to leave. But I wouldn't.

The fact was, I hadn't been with a woman for almost a month. It's called H-O-R-N-Y. And it's also called H-U-M-A-N.

You couldn't have blasted me out of there with plastic explosives. For all my virtuous slavering, I was going to grab the opportunity and run.

No matter how much we lie to ourselves, there's a little bit of Hefner in us all.

She brought me the beer, eyes locked into mine. There was that brief vacuous moment before the first kiss. Her lips were soft and shy.

She moaned low as my hands slid down the curve of her back to her buttocks.

"I lied to you, Stell. I do want to hustle you into bed."

She moaned again, her mouth opening, her tongue tracing the the tip of my tongue. "Well, you've certainly taken your damn sweet time about it."

"Sometimes I think I was a Baptist preacher in another life."

"You've already been a white knight and a psychiatrist. Now I'd just like it if . . . if you were a man. I think that might be half my problem. A man hasn't had me in so long. I feel like there's a dam in me that needs to be burst. And I want it to burst again and again and again and again. . . ."

"Let's not get carried away, lady."

She turned her face up to me sleepily. There was a light smile on her face, and her lips were wet and swollen with kissing. "Let's do," she said. "Let's do get carried away. . . ."

I lifted her in my arms and carried her into the little bedroom. I positioned her belly first on the bed and found a little bottle of body oil on the nightstand. She stretched and moaned like a cat while I stripped the terry-cloth robe away and poured drops of oil down her back.

"A back rub?" she purred.

"For now."

"Does that mean I can return the favor?"

"It does."

"Ummm . . . that feels nice."

"And how does that feel?"

"Oh God . . . that feels wonderful . . . oh, don't stop!"

"I thought I was rubbing your back."

Quickly, she rolled over and began pulling at my buttons and belt feverishly. Her breasts flattened against her chest beneath their own weight, and the fine feminine curve of her hips veed into long silken curls which testified that she was indeed a natural blonde.

I spread the oil across her stomach and thighs as she

84

worked to strip away my clothes. Beneath the touch of my fingers, I felt her nipples rouse and elongate.

"Stand up," she said softly. "Please . . . stand up and turn on the light. I want to see you. I want to look at you."

So I did the lady's bidding—but kept my good side toward her so the scar from a long-ago shark attack would not turn her attention from the matters at hand.

Her hands traced the outline of her own body as she looked at me. "God," she said, "you look so good."

"And you're not so bad yourself, Stell."

"Really? Do you really mean that?"

"If you're done looking, slide over and I'll prove it to you."

She touched herself harder now, massaging her own body. "Yes, Dusky. Now. Prove it to me right now. Prove it to me and be as rough and as fast as you like the first time. We'll have time later for gentleness. I'll give you all the time you want . . . and everything you need. . . ."

《 IX 》

By the fresh light of a September morning, the mangrove trees were eighty feet tall, cliffing abruptly at the water's edge, and the current of the Shark River pressed us onward toward the open Gulf.

The water of the river was deep and dark—but clear. Birds chattered from the depths of the swamp, raccoons foraged in the shallows, and there was the oppressive silence of a wilderness never conquered.

In the depths of that eerie quiet, with no other boats or towns around, it seemed as if the Shark River had transported us through space and time to some South American tributary hellhole that was as beautiful as it was ominous.

That morning I had left Stella Cross asleep, her legs curled against her stomach like a sleeping child.

Lying there in the predawn darkness, she looked confident and unburdened.

And contented.

God knows I had done everything I could do to make her feel content. And it hadn't been easy.

Stella had spent a long lonely year in Flamingo, and we

had loved the night away—she trying to make up for lost time, I just trying to survive.

All her uncertainty had fallen away with her terry-cloth bathrobe, and in the soft bedroom light she had become a tigress. I couldn't release her enough. And she couldn't get enough of me.

After our first three times together, she had cradled my head on her naked breasts, stroking my temple gently.

"Poor Dusky. You didn't know what you were getting yourself into, did you?" she mused.

"No. Guess I'm just lucky."

"And tired?"

"About half and half."

"Can I guess which half?"

"If you can find it."

And she had pressed her lips against my chest, then maneuvered herself over me so that she could trace the line of my stomach and abdomen with her tongue.

"I'm searching," she had said dreamily.

"So I see. Like a needle in a haystack."

And she had laughed. "More like a crowbar in the grass."

And when her mouth found me, she said, "Am I getting warm?"

"One of us is."

"I thought you were tired."

"Maybe this will be my last stand."

"Oh no," she had giggled. "I don't think so. You're so easily . . . discovered. I think you've only just begun to fight. . . ."

And that's the way the whole night went. We had explored and measured and discovered, getting each other's wants and rhythms down until, for a time, it seemed as if we two strangers were one; a joining of all lovers, past, present, and future.

And at long last, when she had finally spent herself, she

had drifted off into sleep. Tired as I was, I had studied her face by the soft glow of the nightstand light, trying to fix the particulars of her in my mind. Maybe it was a form of penitence, but I wanted her to stand out in memory as a living, breathing human being rather than just a one-night bout of climax.

In sleep, the lines disappeared from her face, and she looked very young again. There was a tiny fragment of scar by her left eye—maybe she had been hit by a ball or something when she was a kid. Her lips were a pale brown, thinner than they felt, and her soft white breasts showed a network of blue veins beneath the tissue-paper skin.

How many men had touched those breasts?

How many men had been with this woman?

Too few, that was for sure. And those that had been with her, it seemed, had come only to rob rather than bear gifts.

I had slipped away from her just before dawn, dressed, and written her a note.

I left the note on the pillow beside her:

"Stell, I don't know if I'll ever see you again. But I hope I do. I mean that. Dusky."

So I had walked back to *Sniper* through the sleeping government settlement of Flamingo. White egrets and spoonbills—an Easter-egg pink—hunted the mangrove flats beyond the motel on the low tide. Tree rats rattled in the palms, mosquitoes still swarmed, and Florida Bay was a sheen of mica-colored light in the secret morning darkness.

Surprisingly, Hervey was awake when I arrived.

The cabin of my sportfisherman smelled of coffee and bacon.

"Got plenty of sleep last night, I hope," Hervey had said, giving me an evil grin.

"Don't I look like I got plenty of sleep?"

"Oh, sure, sure. Plenty of sleep in a washing machine, maybe."

So we had gotten an early start, cruising through the dawn stillness of Flamingo Canal to Coot Bay, then through the twisting, turning tributary that we followed to the expanse of Whitewater Bay, where bottlenosed dolphin played before the boat in the shallow water.

In that wilderness maze at the base of Florida, humans and our frail history seem temporary and unimportant. There is a sinister light about the mangrove swamps, as if they are patiently waiting to claim again cities and roads and homes when we have finally blown ourselves into oblivion.

It is a wild giant land of dark water, forbidding islands, and haunting beauty.

I love it.

And so did Hervey.

He stood with me on the flybridge as we snaked our way through a tributary to the broadening Shark River, where the current boiled at glassy intersections. These were the tallest mangrove trees of all now—eighty feet high. The forest along the river was ornate with bromeliads and sea birds, and the only noise was the burble of *Sniper*'s engines and the wind in the high trees.

"This used to be great country," Hervey said. He wore the same jeans and western shirt, and there was a big chew of Red Man in his cheek.

"Used to be?"

"Florida, I mean. You get down in here and you see the way it used to be. Wild, pure—and not just because there ain't any people around. Men used to live here—right on this river, as a matter of fact."

We were midway up the river, and I hadn't seen a single scar of human habitation. "Where in the hell did they live here?"

Hervey motioned toward the south bank. "There. All

along here. My daddy brought me up here when I was a boy. Had a tannic-acid plant right down yonder. Built their houses on stilts. That's my point. People lived here as short as forty years ago—and the Indians for a thousand years before them. But they didn't hurt it none. It's natural for man to live on this earth—but it ain't natural for man to dig deep and dredge it up, change this and alter that just so they can go to their graves rich."

He spit and thought for a moment. "You see, these developers think—no, they damn well *believe*—that Florida ain't nothin' but a property. Something they can buy and sell and own. Well, that's just plain bullshit. No matter what their deeds say or their lawyers tell 'em, they don't *own* no land. They don't own it no more than the Indians did, or we do—or the people a thousand years from now will. We're just tenants. We're renters with a lifetime lease. But they've taken Florida and acted like there ain't gonna be no future. And the way they've treated this state, they might be right."

"I have a feeling you're getting at something."

"You're damn right I am." He paused, working at his chew of tobacco. "You ever been to a development town near Fort Myers called Cape Coral?"

"Flew over it once. About a million miles of dead-end roads and canals, all in nice neat squares. And hardly any trees. From the air, it looks like a big scar."

"Right! And then there's a place like it called Golden Gate, and a couple more just as bad on the east coast. Can't you see? The developers keep pushing right on southward, toward the 'glades. They keep chopping away at Florida, gettin' rich, measurin' how successful they are by the amount of shit they can pile in their own backyard. And they ain't gonna be satisfied until it's all gone." Hervey spit bitterly. "Take my Indian folks, where we're going. Lived there happy as clams for as long as they can remember, and for as long as my granddaddy can remem-

90

ber. Now someone's tryin' to push them off. Tryin' to ruin even that."

"You think developers want that land?"

"Hell, I don't know *who* wants it. It's just that whole way of thinking that pisses me off. People thinkin' the land is something to be bought or sold or stolen. My point is, it's time to fight, damn it. It's time to hunker down and not give in and fight to the last dyin' breath. Because we just ain't fightin' for ourselves."

Hervey was so furious with the slow, sure destruction of the state in which he was born that his bearded face was crimson. "I don't think I've ever seen you so worked up," I said.

He sniffed and looked away, suddenly embarrassed by the long speech he had just made. "I guess it's because, livin' in Key West, I got sort of blind to the trailer parks and the condominiums and that sort of shit. Got so I didn't see it because I didn't want to. But then, a man gets here on the Shark River, which is the way Florida used to be—and could still be, if the developers and the politicians had a brain in their damn heads—and it just sort of brings it all back. Makes me feel stupid, the way I forgot it so easy. And feelin' stupid makes me mad."

"Mad enough to drink a beer?"

He chuckled. "Maybe more than one. I'll get 'em."

He had just turned to go below when I saw it.

At first I thought it was a big palm tree floating in the water. But then I saw the movement of the dragon tail. And the blazing yellow eyes surfaced to watch us pass.

"Jesus, Hervey—look at that!"

He stopped and peered at it. "Goddam! Look at the size of that gator—must be fifteen feet long!"

I brought *Sniper* to idle, letting the current of the river drift us sideways so we could get a better look. "That's no alligator, Hervey. Look at its nose. A gator's nose is round—you know that better than I do. That thing has a pointed nose. It's no gator, Hervey. Can't be. It's a saltwater crocodile."

"My lord," Hervey said softly. "You're right. I've read about them. But I never dreamed I'd ever get the chance to see one. They used to be pretty common when the Spaniards first came to Florida. But now they ain't nowhere—"

"—but here," I finished.

Hervey had been right in his estimation of the croc's size. It swam full on the surface now. It was a full fifteen feet long, and its girth suggested its weight at a half ton. Or more. You could see its massive claws hanging limply beneath it in the clear dark water as it swam, its tail ruddering it slowly across the river.

For the first time in my life, I wished that I owned a camera.

"Can you imagine what woulda happened if we'd decided to stop here and go for a swim?" Hervey said. He still whispered—whispered not because he was afraid of frightening the croc, but because the size and grace and the pure malevolence of the dragon-eyed giant demanded awe.

"Had we gone in here? With the croc?"

"Unless people feed a gator, he ain't aggressive," Hervey said. "Even the big ones will swim away from a man. But a croc—they're somethin' altogether different. Read about them African crocs. They'll stalk a man. They'll hunt him down. If we'd been unlucky enough to swim here, he'da probably taken at least one of us. Maybe both."

The croc paused, motionless in the current. All the way down the river we had been seeing small loggerhead turtles—small meaning thirty- or forty-pounders.

Now he saw one, too.

He submerged soundlessly, without a bit of wasted effort. The turtle was about twenty yards away, his leather-colored head and dull dry eyes studying the surface of the river. Our eyes followed the light wake of the croc as he made his way toward the sea turtle.

"Watch this," Hervey whispered.

He didn't have to nudge me. I was already watching, entranced. Television can't touch the drama of the wilderness—especially when the drama includes something as rare and as huge as that saltwater crocodile.

The loggerhead seemed satisfied that all was well on the Shark River this day; convinced that all was at peace.

He was wrong.

One second, the turtle's head periscoped its way around the surface, and the next second, there was an explosion of water and blood, a brief frenzy upon the river as the croc's head plunged out of the water with the turtle dwarfed within the massive jaws.

And then all was tranquil again except for a light wake which washed against the shore.

"My God almighty," Hervey whistled.

I found that I had been holding my breath. I exhaled and said nothing. I didn't want the search for words to even ripple that image I held of the croc taking the loggerhead. I wanted to hang on to the reverence I felt for as long as I could.

A long time later, when we were far away from the Shark River and with Graveyard Creek and Shark Point well behind us, Hervey finally spoke of it. We were in the Gulf now, riding a light sea in a light September wind, and the water spread away from us tranquil and blue and seemingly endless.

"You know," he said suddenly, "the Indians might have seen that croc in a different light."

"Yeah? What do you mean?"

"Like an omen. Something that unusual—they'd have to think about it as a symbol or something like that."

"And now you're going to tell me what it means as an omen, right?"

"Hell, I don't know what they'd think it meant. You'd have to ask my granddaddy that."

"You think he'd say it was a good omen or a bad omen?"

Hervey smiled. "Ask him tomorrow when you see him." He paused and added, "But whatever kind of omen it is, that croc sure was something to see, wasn't it?"

"It was that."

"If it was all an omen, maybe the people trying to scare my folks off their land are the turtle."

"Or maybe they're the crocodile. And we're the turtle."

Hervey whistled softly. "Damn, I hope not." He whistled again. "That croc scared me—and I'm damn near fearless. . . ."

《 X 》

Panther James and his small clan lived in the clearing of an oak hammock where moss hung from the trees and a blackwater stream moved toward the sawgrass expanse and cypress heads in the distance.

It wasn't what I had expected—not that I'm sure *what* I expected. Watch too many John Wayne movies and you get weird ideas about Indians.

Their little settlement was a combination of the old, the new, and anything else that was comfortable.

We had brought *Sniper* through the mangrove maze of Indian Key Pass in the Ten Thousand Islands to the old coastal town of Everglades City. Everglades City looks like a small New England village built, strangely, on that rare high ground between swamp and sea. The houses there are made of wood, neat and well cared for, and the roads are wide and empty, lined with the old glass-globed streetlights.

We had an early supper at the Rod and Gun Club, a landmark of old Florida grace, then hunted up a rental car.

"You sure your boat's going to be okay here?" Hervey

had asked. "I'd feel real bad if something happened to it while you were doing a favor for me."

"Do you know what the crime rate is in this little town?"

"Next to nothing, I'd guess."

"Right. Besides, I'm going to moor her downriver. A friend of mine here named Bill Williams said I could use his dock. He'll keep an eye on things. You call your folks?"

"Can't. No phone. My young aunt—Myrtle James Cougar's her name—always calls me from the Indian school where she works. But they'll have food waiting for us. You can bet on that. Granddaddy Panther James always knows when people are coming."

I eyed him for a moment to see if he was serious. "Do you believe that?"

He grinned. "I'm part Indian myself, remember."

Our rental car was a red Ford that smelled of cigar. The lady at the desk didn't like our not having a credit card. They want everyone to believe that plastic currency is a modern necessity—like fingerprints, a Social Security number, and a political affiliation. The retail hawks try to make you feel uncomfortable if you can't—or won't—produce a credit card upon demand. The commercials tell you they're the key to financial freedom. In truth, they're plastic rungs on the ladder into debt.

So we paid her cash in advance, rolled down the windows, turned the air on high, and drove on out of Everglades City, past the old train depot which has become the Captain's Table motel and restaurant, and turned east on the Tamiami Trail.

The Trail is the two-lane asphalt strip which arrows through the Everglades connecting Naples, on the west coast of Florida, with Miami.

It was the road which Grafton McKinney had told us

about—the one which he had worked on with Panther James, Hervey's grandfather.

Driving across it a couple of hours before sunset, it was easy to imagine the way it had been. The trail is a desolate eighty miles of highway now. Back then, when it was only swamp and snakes, gators and mosquitoes, it must have been hell.

At fifty-five miles an hour, we headed inland. Sawgrass stretched away from us on both sides of the road, where vultures fed on the highway carnage of bloated possums and armadillos. In the far distance were cypress heads, cool and inviting in the late-afternoon heat. The land was low and endless, and you could see the shadows of clouds passing over the sawgrass two miles away.

The traffic was light—but fast. Cars barely paused to pass us.

"Kinda bleak out here from the road," Hervey said. He was driving, spitting out the window.

He was right. Every few miles a rickety billboard would scream at you in multi-color letters:

Indian Camp Ahead
Alligator Wrestling
Souvenirs

Or:

Airboat Rides Next Right
See Florida Panthers, Rare Snakes

And a few miles beyond the sign we would pass some dilapidated roadside Indian camp with a wooden fence and thatched roofs with television antennas protruding— or some rural Everglades concession with junked cars piled by the blackwater canal where the airboats were tethered with their huge airplane propellers.

The hammocks of human inhabitation all seemed

97

rather grim and desperate on their frail roadside footholds against the enormous background of the sawgrass.

"You got to get back in to really see the Everglades," Hervey said.

"Any chance of our getting back in?"

He grinned. "We're going to stay with my granddaddy, ain't we? You can't get no further in than that."

That was almost an understatement.

Just before the border of the Big Cypress National Park reservation, Hervey signaled and slowed.

"Where in the hell are you turning?"

"On that road, of course."

"Road? I don't see any road."

"You ain't looking close enough."

Sure enough, just ahead was a little clearing in the sawgrass at the edge of a pretty circle of hatrack cypress. A narrow plank bridge crossed a stream and disappeared into the swamp.

"That bridge doesn't look like it would hold my weight—let alone the weight of a car."

Hervey shrugged. "Aunt Myrtle says she drives the pickup across it every day. But damn if I don't think you're right. That bridge does look a little old and poorly."

Hervey turned and idled the car onto the planking. You could feel it bow beneath the weight of the car. Once across, he exhaled softly.

"Wouldn't want to try that too often."

"And never on a full stomach. I think one more pound would have done us in."

The bridge exited onto a narrow dirt road that looked more like a wagon trail. White ibis flushed from the myrtle flats before us, and a swallow-tailed kite—looking like a combination of hawk and dove—was lovely and pale against the September sun.

Gator, the big Chesapeake, sat in the back seat and

whined with the appearance of every bird, anxious to be after it.

After about twenty miles on the dirt path, the road branched at the perimeter of a cypress swamp where the trees were laden with moss. In the middle of the road, one of the biggest rattlesnakes I've ever seen took his time getting out of the way.

"The Johnny Egret family lives off to the right there," Hervey said. "Maybe we can pay them a visit tomorrow."

"Sounds good. How much farther?"

"Not long." Hervey smiled. "Too much farther and we'll be back on the Shark River again."

The road began to curve, oak trees hanging down over the path, and we came around a bend to the camp of Hervey's maternal relatives.

A couple of small cur dogs came yapping out to meet us. In the middle of the oak hammock was a dirt clearing. An open pole house with a palmetto thatch roof—a chickee—was built in the center of the clearing. Smoke drifted from a hole in the thatching, and a large cast-iron pot simmered over the coals of a fire. To the left was another thatched chickee—but this one had walls. An old school bus without tires rusted in the weeds behind the hut, and to the right was a neat plank house with a porch and screen doors. A Chevy pickup truck that looked as if it had seen as many years as miles was parked beside the shack in the shade.

"Looks like Myrtle's home," Hervey said simply.

As we got out of the car, a heavyset Indian woman of about thirty came out to meet us. She wore a simple blue pleated skirt, white blouse, and sandals. She wore her hair in a bun.

"We were about to give up on you two!"

"And how's my youngest aunt?"

She came up smiling and hugged Hervey, then held out her hand to me while we were introduced. I noticed a

99

little girl with jet-black hair and eyes like an owl's hiding behind a big oak.

"That's my daughter Eisa, Mr. MacMorgan. She's a little shy of strangers. We don't get many visitors out here. And lately the ones we do get aren't very nice."

"Maybe we can help change that, Myrtle. And my name's Dusky."

While Hervey and I got our sparse luggage out of the rental car, the Chesapeake didn't waste any time letting the cur dogs know who was going to be in charge while he was around. He rolled the one lean cur foolish enough the challenge him, then lifted his leg and urinated on the fallen dog. After a few tense minutes of sniffing and growling, the other dogs decided it was safer to accept him. While the Chesapeake trotted off to explore the grounds, the three curs fell into line behind, wagging their tails, happy to have a leader.

"Granddad Panther around?" Hervey asked.

Myrtle nodded, suddenly uncomfortable. "He's over in his chickee. But before you see him, Hervey, I'd like to talk to you. Are you hungry?"

We weren't, but we accepted supper anyway. We ate sitting on a pole platform in the kitchen hut. She served us a stew of feral pork and tomatoes in stoneware bowls, fry bread, and a thick drink made of corn she called sofki. I liked everything but the sofki, so I drank it as quickly as possible to save her any embarrassment.

While she served us, she talked. She had a soft low voice edged with worry. There was a steadfast quality about her that put me in mind of April.

I decided that I liked her.

She said, "Hervey, you haven't seen Papa in a while— that's why I wanted to talk with you first."

Hervey looked concerned. "Is he sick?"

"Oh no," she said quickly. "For his age, he's as healthy as they come. He was eighty-seven last June, you know."

She paused for a moment, trying to speak carefully. "It's just that since we've had all these problems around here, he's gone a little different in the head. Not crazy—just different. He's got strange ideas and he's been saying some pretty strange things. He won't even go back to the burial mound anymore. For some reason, he's got it fixed in his mind that it's his fault someone has been digging there. And when Eisa turned up missing, he just knew that she was dead and that it was his fault. It all has something to do with this swamp-monster business. He's convinced the ancestors have sent the swamp monster to punish us—the monster and the fires and everything else."

"Hummm," said Hervey. "It's not like him to be scared. Or maybe it's just the way I remember him. I used to think he wasn't afraid of anything."

"Oh, he's not frightened. It's . . . more like he's just *resigned* to it. It's like he wants to give himself up to die before we are forced to leave. He doesn't want to eat, and the only person he wants to see is Eisa. He's crazy about Eisa."

The little girl had changed her hiding place. Now she peered around the corner at us from the back of the chickee. I gave her a big wink and heard her giggle as she ducked back into hiding.

"I can see why," I said.

Hervey put down his empty stew bowl. "Have you had any more trouble since you talked to me last?"

She nodded. "The day before yesterday. Eisa and I were off at school. I don't know where my husband was. I got home and Papa was standing outside staring up at the sun." Her voice trembled slightly, as if about to cry. "It was awful, the look on his face. He said he had seen the creature again. He said that it was hunting Eisa. He said he wanted the sun to burn his eyes because that was the only way to make the creature leave us alone."

Hervey had that strange deadly look on his face again. "You know there's no swamp monster, Myrtle. You know it's just someone trying to scare you out of here."

"I don't know what to believe anymore, Hervey! It's easy for you to laugh at it and not believe, because you've never been here alone at night and heard your daughter wake up screaming, dreaming about that thing. And you've never seen the tracks it makes!"

"Any chance of us seeing them now?" I asked.

She inhaled, gathering herself. "Day before yesterday, it must have gone into our house. It left more handprints. I didn't wash them off because I knew you were coming."

We followed her across the clearing to the plank shack. The screen door slammed behind us. Inside it was dark and cool. There was a bare wooden table, a shelf full of books, and oil lamps on the wall. The place smelled of damp earth and dish soap.

The house had two simple bedrooms. Above the double bed was a picture of Jesus in a cheap gold frame. There was an ashtray on one nightstand and an open book on the other. In Eisa's room was a narrow single bed beneath a red spread. There were crayon pictures drawn by a child tacked to the wall.

"There are the handprints," Myrtle said simply. "The creature left those again."

The ceiling was about ten feet high. Just below the joining of roof and wall was the massive outline of a human hand. It was printed in a gray marl.

There was a wooden chair beside the bed. I studied the surface of the chair before climbing up to get a better look at the handprint.

It was three times the size of my hand—and I have big hands.

"Now are you convinced?" Myrtle said.

"I'm convinced someone is going to a lot of trouble to scare you," I said.

I pointed to the handprint. "Was the print made with the same kind of mud last time?"

She thought for a moment. "Yes. I think so. Why?"

"That kind of mud—the gray marl kind. Is it common around her?"

"Well, now that I think about it, no. I don't think so. The creek bottom is all sand."

"And wet sand doesn't make much of a print when it dries."

Hervey said, "Could you tell if someone used that chair to put the print that high?"

"No. Not for sure. There was no mud on it. But they could have wiped it off when they were done. To get their hands in that kind of mud, they had to get their feet in it too."

"Unless whatever made it really is eight feet tall," Myrtle said.

"You've never seen it, right?"

She shook her head. "Just Papa. And Eisa, of course."

"How did Eisa describe it?"

Myrtle searched around the room for a moment. Finally, she pointed to one of the crayon drawings on the wall. "I had her make a picture of it. She draws real good for her age. People at the school say I should encourage her. They say there are too few Indian artists."

All the other drawings on the wall were multicolored; bright and springlike, filled with a child's imagination. In contrast, she had drawn the swamp monster in stark blacks and browns.

I studied it closely.

She had given the creature a pointed black head. Brown scribbles suggested hair. It walked erect, upright. It had short arms, but huge hands. There was a half-moon frown on a face loaded with fangs.

"Has she said much about it—being carried away by that thing?"

Myrtle's eyes moistened. "No . . . hardly at all. She just said it didn't hurt her. She doesn't like to talk about it. But she still has those dreams. Those nightmares. . . ."

Hervey put his arm around his mother's youngest sister. He had that look on his face again. "Myrtle, I promise you—we're going to find the character that's doing this. And when we do, he's gonna wish he was never born."

"Oh, I hope so, Hervey. I can't stand much more. I really can't. . . ."

≪ XI ≫

The old Indian, Panther James, was in his chickee, sitting on the dirt floor in the darkness.

There was a blanket over the doorway, and when Hervey pulled it open the setting sun filtered in like a dim spotlight. It turned the leather face and hawk nose to gold.

Panther James had the eyes of an old and weary hound. But also in the eyes was the glimmer of shrewdness, or humor, or maybe some great knowledge. He wore a long-sleeved blouse sewn of blue and red and yellow rag cloth, patterned into horizontal bands. His big bare feet protruded from his baggy jeans, and on his head, tilted jauntily, was a brim hat molded by rain and sweat and the years.

When we ducked into the chickee, he looked up blinking like a turtle. Then his face broke into a big toothless smile.

"Is that my grandson?"

"It's good to see you again, Granddad."

They embraced, smacking each other on the back.

"You've gotten fatter. That daughter of mine must be treating you good, huh?"

"And you've lost more teeth."

The old man laughed. Suddenly he glanced down at the cheap wristwatch he was wearing. I noticed that the sweep hand wasn't moving, and the hour hand had been broken off.

"What took you so long?" he said.

"We came by boat. And since when do you wear a watch?"

"I stole it."

"Sure."

"It's true. I gave a man in Ochopee some dollar bills and he gave me this fine thing. He seemed not to mind being cheated."

"I bet."

"It made an awful ticking noise at first, but I have since fixed it. The ticking would wake me up at night and the face of it would glow like a green eye. Now it just glows." The old man studied me for a moment. "Who's this blond man?"

"A friend, Granddad. He came with me to help."

Panther James said something in a guttural singsong language I did not understand. Hervey shook his head. "You have to speak English, Granddad. I don't understand."

"When you were a boy you understood. In the summer months when you came to stay. I taught you, remember?"

Hervey smiled. "I was smarter when I was younger."

"We all are. Only this watch has gotten smarter as it aged." He looked at me again. "I told my stupid grandson that I had seen you in a dream."

"Me?"

"Yes. I saw you in this dream"—he looked at the watch again—"maybe a week ago. Yes, a week ago. You were in the water fighting a creature with many teeth.

You thought that it was a shark. But it wasn't a shark. It left you with a very handsome scar. You killed it. I was very impressed."

I thought about the big dusky shark which had attacked me many years ago while in SEAL training.

"Something like that happened."

"The scar is on your side?"

I nodded.

"It wasn't a shark?"

"No—it was a shark, all right."

The old man looked confused. And then he just shrugged. "Oh well. My dreams aren't what they used to be." He looked at Hervey. "I'm glad to see you, grandson, but this thing you have come to help us fight—it is useless."

"Maybe. Maybe not. Dusky and I think your swamp monster is just a man dressed up trying to scare you off your land."

He shrugged, resigned. "Think what you will. But I am telling you the truth. It is a punishment, don't you see? We have been entrusted with the care of our land. But we have failed that trust. The consequences are inevitable. We must lose the land."

"Just because some artifact hunters dug into your burial mound? Granddad—don't give up so easily."

Panther James gave a wry smile. "My daughter Myrtle told you that. Am I right? Her brain has become very simple since she began going to the government schools." He shook his head. "My great sadness is that Eisa must become so simple. They require that things fit the words in their books. They must see a rock as a rock and a tree as a tree, and food as food. They refuse to see any farther because then it will not fit their words." He paused. "These men destroying our burial grounds—they are only messengers. They are just the symbol of our final failure. Just as the swamp creature is a messenger."

The old man wiped his face, looking concerned for the first time. "That bothers me more than anything else," he said. "The swamp creature hunts our little Eisa. I find myself wanting to fight it, but I know I cannot."

"That's why we're here, Granddad. We'll make sure it doesn't bother Eisa."

He made an empty motion with his hands. "Try if you like—but it is useless. Can't you see? Eisa is the last of us—the very last of the pure Tequesta. Myrtle can have no more children. Her husband has been ruined by whiskey. And that leaves only Eisa. That's why he hunts only her. For the generations before the whites came, our people built the mounds here and cared for the land. Now their blood runs only in little Eisa. And when he takes her, we will all be dead. The ancestors, me, the land—everything."

"But Granddad, if the creature wanted to kill Eisa, why didn't he do it when he took her the first time?"

Panther James thought for a moment. "Damned if I know," he said.

"Then at least let us try. We'll watch the burial mound tonight. Have they been digging lately?"

"Oh, yes. They dig every night. I feel their shovels in my stomach." He snorted. "Myrtle says it is just indigestion, but I know better." He looked at me again. "Is old Grafton McKinney a friend of yours?"

"How did you know that?"

Panther James hooted softly, smiling. He looked at Hervey. "See there—I can still see some things." And to me he added, "He's the man who shits and runs from snakes. And he thought *I* was stupid! I have seen him in my dreams many times. I am sorry that he will die soon. I liked him very much." And then Panther James turned his old dark eyes on me. "And you too, blond man. I am sorry that you too will die in not so many years. I admired the way you fought the creature that scarred your side. . . ."

Myrtle told us to store our gear in Eisa's room. She followed us around the yard like a kitten, playing her shy-eyed game. She would hide, and when I caught her watching us I would wink and she would giggle.

"She's a little beauty," I told Hervey.

"Reminds me of April when she was little."

"I'm trying to picture what kind of lowlife bastard it would take to scare a harmless little girl like her."

"When we find him we'll ask him. If I don't wring his head off first."

"You may have to wait in line."

It was a warm September twilight. White ibis flew in rough arrow formation toward the setting sun, and bullfrogs croaked from the swamp in a rumbling chorus.

There was a freshness to the air there in the Everglades. There was the odor of spring water and the clean sage smell of cypress. Every breeze that came through the cypress beyond the oak hammock leached a certain cool musk from the land.

While Hervey talked about family and things with Myrtle, I changed in Eisa's room. The handprint had been scrubbed away. I pulled on the soft Limey commando pants and my Special Forces boots, oiled glove-soft, then decided on a plain black knit T-shirt in favor of the warmer Navy watch sweater.

While I dressed, I thought about the old man. He had impressed me. While his mind seemed to have gone a bit awry—as Myrtle had said—he was still right on the mark with some of the things he had said. Like most people, I'd like to believe that there are people who have a sixth sense about the past. And the future. Maybe because it implies some order in the scheme of things. But there's a pragmatic side to me that scoffs at the few bits of proof

I've acquired over the years. He had mentioned the shark attack. How had he known that? Or that Graff McKinney was a friend. My pragmatic side insisted that Hervey had probably mentioned it to Myrtle at some time over the years. And she had told the old man.

But what about his last prediction?

Only my own death would prove him right on that.

When I was ready, I met Hervey outside on the porch.

"You bring a weapon with you?" he asked.

I touched the Randall attack/survival knife strapped to my side. "Just this. I thought you had the shotgun."

"I do. But I'm leaving it with Myrtle. She doesn't know when her husband's going to be back. And the thoughtless bastard carries their rifle with him." Hervey gave a long shrill whistle, and in a few moments the huge Chesapeake came crashing through the brush into the clearing. "If we get into any rough stuff, Gator will be some help."

"After seeing him in action last night, I'd say he'll be all the help we could possibly need. Unless the artifact hunters have automatic weapons."

"And a lot of them at that."

I followed Hervey through the oak hammock along the darkwater stream. We carried flashlights and mosquito netting. While we moved along the edge of the creek I watched closely for tracks.

To make mud, the guy in the swamp-monster costume had to get his hands wet.

And to get his hands wet he had to get his feet wet.

Still, I found no tracks.

No human tracks, anyway. But the creek bed was alive with every other kind of print: deer, coon, wading birds, feral hog—and even the massive paw print of a Florida bear.

It was a silvery twilight in the Everglades. The cypress

head in the distance looked cooler and darker. In the weakening light, sawgrass on the far horizon looked like pastureland.

The burial mound was about three miles from the main camp. We had to cross the stream to get to it. There was another oak hammock—this one older, and with much bigger trees. In the middle of the hammock was a striking line of elevation. It looked as if someone had dumped several thousand tons of pure sand there, then planted the top and walls with small shrubs, palmetto, and oaks.

The oaks beside the mound were massive, with limbs like beams, and the silver tinge of dusk painted the mound in a celestial light. At both ends of the hammock were royal poinciana trees, like giant umbrellas, shading the burial center with a mass of late lavender blooms.

I am not the religious type, but there was a venerable air about the burial mound.

"Sure is pretty back in here," I said.

"Yeah," said Hervey, swatting at some mosquitoes. He pointed to the largest oak tree at the base of the mound. "Back when I was a kid, I built a pole house in the tree. Stayed out here a couple of days by myself."

"Your granddad didn't mind?"

"Mind? Hell, he helped me. Fell out of the tree house once and liked to broke his ass. He's always been a wild old character—once you get to know him. Folks who don't know him usually think he's deaf and dumb—like Graff McKinney." Hervey kicked at something in the sand, bent down, and lifted a chunk of pottery shard. "See this here? Might be a thousand years old. When I was a kid, I used to try and imagine all the ceremonies that went on here. And after a real hard rain, you could find bits of bone. Once part of a human skull rolled right down the mound at my feet. I'd always bury them back. Didn't want to piss off any of the ancestors, you know."

"I don't see any signs of digging," I said.

"Me neither. Let's walk around to the other side. Maybe they've been doing their graverobbing over there. There's an old swamp buggy path that curves in only about a half mile away on that side. It's the most likely spot."

It was indeed the most likely spot.

In contrast to the other side of the massive burial mound, the west bank was a mass of recently dug trenches.

Not small tidy trenches, either.

It looked as if they had brought a backhoe in to expedite their desecration.

The trenches burrowed fifteen or twenty feet toward the heart of the mound. The offal had been thrown haphazardly at the base. A recent rain had filled the shallowest trenches with water. The robbers had thrown their beer cans and cigarette wrappers on the ground.

The west side of the mound looked like a construction site where kids went to have their beer parties.

"Son of a bitch," Hervey said.

I had no personal interest in the land—or the mound—but the indignity of it was enough to make anybody with a sense of right and wrong mad.

"The world has its good people. But it does seem to have more than its share of assholes and jerks."

Hervey slammed his gear down on the ground. "And what the hell do they get out of this?" he demanded. "They get a few beads. And they get a couple of shoeboxes full of bones so they can leave them on the mantelpiece and prove to their scruffy-assed friends what experts they are on Indian culture. If they really cared about Indian culture, would they do this kind of shit?"

It wasn't a question that demanded an answer. While Hervey fumed, I got to work picking out a recon point for the two of us. At the top of the mound was a gathering of heavy vegetation. The sand was beach-soft and damp.

"I think we ought to split up. If they do show up tonight, we'll give them plenty of time to do some digging."

"What?"

"Just take it easy, Hervey. You brought me along to help, remember. When it comes to fixing boats and running reefs, you're the best. But this sort of thing falls into my line of expertise."

Hervey nodded, pulling at his beard. "Sorry. Okay, you run the show. But why give them a chance to do more digging?"

"Because I want to hear what they have to say while they dig. If they've been trying to scare your folks out, they'll sure as hell mention it. Maybe even joke about it. Remember, we can't just assume these graverobbers are behind it all. Right?"

"I guess that's so."

"Okay. You keep the dog with you. Make yourself comfortable in that palmetto thicket on top of the mound. We'd better just plan on sleeping here tonight and every other night until they come back."

"And what if it is these guys who are playing this swamp-monster game—the ones who stole Eisa?"

I cupped my hands together and blew between my thumbs. "I'll make an owl call when I think it's time to go in. You just follow my lead. If you hear that call, you'll know I've got it set so they can't get away. If they are the ones who took Eisa, you'll have a chance to soften them up as much as you want before we take them to the law."

"And if they're not?"

"Then we'll make sure they'll never ever even think about coming back here."

"Now I wish I'd brought the shotgun," Hervey murmured. "I had no idea they'd done this much damage."

I looked into my old friend's face. "Hervey, from the look in your eyes, I'm glad you didn't bring it. This old mound has seen enough death. And I'm no gravedigger. . . ."

« XII »

They came by jeep long before midnight. There were five of them.

At first I thought it was just a matter of our getting lucky. I'd planned on having to stake out the burial mound for a lot longer.

But then I realized that it was Saturday night. And artifact hunters do most of their dirty work on Saturday nights and Sunday mornings. I remembered what old Panther James had said about feeling their shovels in his stomach. Maybe they had been coming every night all along. Maybe they were hunting for something in particular.

I heard the rumble of the jeep bouncing down the swamp-buggy trail first. And then there was a brief flare of headlights as they swept through the undergrowth.

Bullfrogs paused in their chorus. And somewhere a small animal squealed with finality.

"I think we've got company." Hervey's voice was ghostly from the darkness at the top of the mound.

"Let's be good hosts—until I give you the signal."

"Take your time. I'm getting real neighborly with a snake up here that's almost big enough to incorporate."

"A rattler?"

"Naw. Indigo, I think. Moccasins probably ate all the rattlers up here."

Hervey wasn't exaggerating much about the snake population around the mound. I had counted two ground rattlers and one full-grown diamondback as I made my way to the big oak where Hervey had once built a tree house. And once safely high in its limbs, I could hear snakes moving through the palmettos below.

"You don't worry about your dog with all these snakes around?"

And from the top of the mound, Hervey answered, "He's swamp-smart, remember? Gives 'em a wide berth. And Dusky, you just gave me a great idea."

I didn't have a chance to ask him what the idea was. The jeep came ambling through the brush in low gear, and for one wild moment I thought their headlights had nailed my position in the tree.

But they said nothing. Three of them were dim shapes in the back of the jeep. I could see the faces of the other two by the squint-eyed cigarette glow.

These were no rookie artifact hunters. And it obviously wasn't the first time they had visited this mound. They had car headlights mounted on poles and connected to twelve-volt batteries. They placed three of the lights around the perimeter of their excavation.

It put the mound in an icy white glare. While the rest of them unloaded shovels and coolers of beer, another assembled a big wooden frame that held two levels and two sizes of screen mesh—an obvious sieve.

The driver was the ostensible leader. He was a hugely fat man who handled himself with the pompous air of someone who believes that size suggests power. His T-shirt was sweat-stained, and he kept a cigarette stuck in the corner of his mouth.

The other four were a mixed bag: ages twenty-five to maybe forty. They chortled a lot and hit the beer in the cooler hard. They seemed delighted with what they were doing.

While the fat man sifted, the other four shoveled. Each man had his own trench. It was clear that they planned on digging straight through to the other side of the mound. It also became clear they were all telephone-company employees from Palmville, north of Naples.

Working on their failing phone system was a pastime.

Desecrating Indian graves was their passion.

I gave them an hour to hang themselves. I waited patiently high in the tree, hoping they would mention their scheme to scare Panther James off his land.

But they never did.

They bragged about other mounds they had robbed. They spoke of artifacts and tribes with the air of the pseudoscientist. They dug and talked, joked about their mistresses, and drank a hell of a lot of beer.

I worried about Hervey sitting atop the mound. Him and his dog—I didn't know which would be the hardest to control.

Once I heard a big animal trot through the brush between me and the jeep, and I thought the two of them had tired of waiting and were going in for the kill.

What finally convinced me it was time to act was when the men did start talking about Panther James's swamp monster. I had cupped my hands to my ears, not wanting to miss a word.

The fat man was talking. "Eddie there says he saw the tracks—isn't that right, Eddie?"

"Like I said before—I brought my wife and kids down

here yesterday afternoon after work. She thought I'd been sneakin' out to see Alice, and I just wanted to prove that we was down here workin'."

"Be the first time you was telling her the truth, Eddie," one of them chided.

"You want me to tell this story or don't you? I was about to tell you how my little boy started yellin' for me. Thought he was snakebit. I went after him on a run, and when I got there he was standing there with his mouth open, pointing at his track. You guys ain't seen nothing like it." He stopped shoveling for a moment and held his hands three feet apart. "I swear to God, it was this big. Looked like a barefooted man's footprint, only a hell of a lot wider. If the Swamp Ape didn't make it, I don't want to meet the man who did."

The other men kidded him for a while. He promised to find it for them later. Most of them believed. A couple didn't. They jabbered on about the Swamp Ape, and then flying saucers as they picked the beads and bones from the mound—the fat man sticking them in the bucket like a vulture selecting the best from a bloated corpse.

So that's what convinced me to move in.

It was obvious they didn't know a damn thing about the plot to chase Panther James out.

They were just a mindless few among the hundreds of thousands who move through this life selfishly and stupidly. They filled me with a sense of the pathetic, and it drained my anger away. There are too many out there like these men. They live a random existence without a love of truth and without a code of personal honor. They can rationalize any act, any deed, because they believe the only law they must embrace is public law. Anything that won't get them arrested—or get them a stern warning from their preacher—must be all right.

They're like kids who get too used to the grown-ups' making the rules.

And they never learn—or maybe never want to learn—that the time comes when any thinking human being makes his own rules.

So I just wanted to get it over as quickly as possible.

Only one thing bothered me. The fat man was the only one armed. He wore a western-style .22-caliber revolver in a holster.

And I knew that men like these don't go to the woods unarmed.

Before whistling for Hervey, I climbed down out of the tree and made my way to their jeep. Had they been responsible for stealing little Eisa, I would have disabled the jeep. Instead, I hunted for weapons.

They were easy to find. There were three shotguns and a rifle protruding from the back.

I took them and dropped them into the creek beyond the trail they had forged.

That left only the fat man to worry about.

I made my way back to the perimeter of darkness around the mound. The fat man was still sifting away, stopping only long enough to gulp a beer and light another cigarette. He threw the empty cans in the brush with the others.

The only cover behind him was a small myrtle tree. I mapped a plan in my mind, then gave Hervey the owl call I had promised.

By the time Hervey made himself seen, I was behind the fat man, hunkered down by the little tree.

Hervey is big and bearlike by normal light. But in the stark white glare of the work lamps, he looked positively fearsome.

And at his side, the yellow-eyed Chesapeake snarled like some hound from hell.

One by one, the men went silent. And one by one they followed their neighbor's gaze to Hervey.

He stood on the top of the mound, black beard blazing,

as if he were about to make a sermon. In his right hand he held a chunk of hatrack cypress. It was more club than walking stick. The four men held their shovels tightly as they backed themselves toward the shadows. Only the fat man stood his ground. His voice was a surprising falsetto, like that of an adolescent boy.

"You got business here?" he said darkly.

Hervey began to work his way down the mound. "Yeah," he said. "My business is to make you put the stuff you found back in the mound. And then you're going to cover it all back up nice and neat, and take them beer cans and leave. And if I ever catch you back here, lard-ass, I'm gonna tear your head off and use it for a doorstop."

The fat man looked at his four accomplices for reassurance—or maybe just to make sure they were still there.

He said, "Those are pretty big words for one man."

Hervey snorted. "I figure one man is all it'll take with five lard-asses like you."

I had been watching the fat man's right hand. He was moving it ever so slowly toward his holster. I wanted to make sure I timed it right.

There was no room for a mistake. Hervey had backed them in a corner a little too quickly. He had frightened them a little too much—and frightened men turn deadly all too readily.

Just as the fat man unsnapped the holster latch, I ducked through the brush and grabbed his meaty hand. I thought the surprise of being taken from behind would stop him if nothing else.

It didn't. He was pretty quick for his weight.

His reflexes were good. But his judgment was bad. Very bad.

When I grabbed him by the wrist, he whirled away from me and sent a big overhand left toward my jaw. It was like ducking a tank.

I felt the fist bluster harmlessly past my left ear. He had small piggish blue eyes. They held the wild look of a renegade horse as he threw another punch at me, and still another.

Both missed.

And he suddenly looked very worried.

I was tired of dialogue. And besides, his revolver was still in the holster. I doubled him over with a lancing fist to the solar plexus, then caught him with a solid elbow at the intersection of neck and jaw.

There was a jello-like repercussion when the bulk of him landed on the ground.

He looked up at me like a fat little boy, and for a second I thought he was going to cry.

"Watch out!"

It was Hervey's voice. And I didn't waste time asking any questions. I ducked, dove, and rolled—just as I heard the toy crack of small-caliber pistol fire.

I had been wrong. The fat man wasn't the only one carrying a side arm. A tall lanky guy had materialized a revolver—from his pocket, probably.

He had a dazed look on his face, trying to level the weapon on me.

But he never got a chance to fire again.

The big retriever covered the base of the mound in three Homeric bounds, then crashed his considerable weight into the guy with the gun.

The revolver went off again. And again—but aimed harmlessly at the night sky.

Some instinct told the dog to lock onto the guy's right arm.

And he did—hair bristling, white teeth slashing.

Hervey got to him, took the gun, then called off his dog. Gator heeled obediently, but still snarled at his fallen adversary.

Hervey motioned with the revolver. "You boys are a

little out of your league here. You best start covering up these holes like I told you."

"Jesus, that dog 'bout ripped my arm off!" The lanky guy beheld his bleeding wrist with a stare of terror.

He was right. It didn't look good.

"Let's just let them go, Hervey."

"Let them go! Not until these bastards have put back some of that dirt!"

"That guy's arm is pretty bad, Hervey. And fat boy here might have a concussion."

"We won't never come back," one of them said quickly.

"They don't enforce no laws about digging Indian mounds in Florida," another of them added. "We just didn't know it was your property." And to Hervey's steely look, he added, "It's our fault. We shoulda asked."

Hervey spit with disgust. "Okay, okay. Go. You bastards make me sick, and I swear to God—if I ever hear about you digging mounds within a hundred miles of here, I'll hunt you down. Each and every one of you. You can bet your lives on it. And you will be."

They didn't hesitate.

They left their shovels and their lamps and their sieve.

Even the fat man found his feet and scrambled, lest Hervey change his mind and set the dog on them again.

There was a strange look on Hervey's face. He seemed to cock his head and listen expectantly. I was about to ask why when I heard the jeep start—and then heard a chorus of swearing and a muffled scream.

Then Hervey smiled. "I guess they found the snake."

"You didn't stick a rattler in there with them, did you?"

"Naw. Couldn't find a rattler. And I looked. Had to settle on the indigo. Where are those pit vipers when you need them?"

I studied him for a moment, trying to figure out if he

really would have stuck a rattler in the jeep. He sensed my question, and the smile disappeared from his face.

He said, "Dusky, what would you do if strangers came into your house and started wrecking the place looking for things that are family keepsakes?"

"I see what you mean."

"I know the only thing Indian about me is my mother. It ain't that. It's a matter of *family*. Those jerks were robbing from my family. So you're damn right I was hunting for a rattlesnake. I'da done it, too."

There was one more wild oath before the jeep roared off through the swamp. I smiled. "I think the indigo was effective enough."

Hervey chuckled. "It'll be a cold day before they come back, I reckon." He put his hands on his hips and surveyed the trenches in the family mound. "Think we can wait until tomorrow before we start cleaning up here?"

I didn't get a chance to answer.

That's when we heard the muffled echo of a shotgun blast.

And then the frightened cry of a woman, her anguish seeping through the Everglades darkness. . . .

《 XIII 》

My flashlight threw a frail beam through the night.

Above, the tropical stars pierced the light-years, cold and clear and unconcerned with the petty struggling of two men running through the swamps on distant Earth.

For his age, Hervey was in pretty good shape.

Even so, he was no runner, and he was soon lagging far behind.

I was at a disadvantage—that being I didn't know where the hell I was or which way I was going. If you've ever been in the 'glades at night, you know how easy it is to get turned around.

I noticed that the Chesapeake, Gator, was sticking just ahead of me. Every now and then, when I made a wrong turn, he'd wait a moment until I had corrected my error, then start out again.

Finally, I realized how stupid I was being. All I had to do was follow him. He knew how to get back to the house.

When I finally came chugging into the clearing, all the oil lamps were burning brightly in the little plank house. Myrtle stood on the porch in a flannel night dress. She held the sawed-off shotgun in both hands. When she saw me, she raised it as if about to shoot.

"Whoa there, lady!"

"Dusky? Dusky, is that you?"

"Yeah. It's me—and if you'll lower that twelve-gauge . . ."

"Oh, I'm sorry!"

I went running up to the porch. She let me take the shotgun, then buried her face in her hands, crying.

"Eisa—is Eisa okay?"

"Yes, thank God. But that . . . that thing came back tonight. Oh, it was so awful. I was in bed but I wasn't asleep, and I heard this heavy breathing and I looked up, and . . . and, oh my God . . ."

She broke into uncontrollable sobs.

Hervey came wheezing into the clearing as I tried to comfort her. I told him what had happened.

"Where's Granddad?" he asked.

"In his chickee, I suppose. He didn't even come out when I shot."

"Did you hit it?"

She shook her head. "I don't know. It was all like a bad dream. It was just standing there, looking at me. I grabbed the gun, and then it started to run away. I went to Eisa's room to make sure she was okay. That's all I could think about—that it had gotten Eisa. But she was still sleeping, and I ran outside and it was just going through the trees toward the cypress head. I pulled both triggers, and then I screamed for you. I don't know if I hit it or not."

"Granddad," Hervey said. "Let's make sure he's okay."

The two of us went running toward the chickee. There was an oil lamp burning inside. Panther James sat on the dirt floor, naked but for his weathered hat and the multi-colored shirt.

He looked up when we came in. "I can't find my pants," he said.

"That thing was back, Granddad."

The old man looked at the broken watch. "Right on time," he said. "I've got to find those damn pants."

"You stay here, Granddad. Dusky and I are going to go after it."

"Won't do any good," he said flatly. "It wants Eisa, but maybe it'll take me. I'll go find it and speak with it. But I don't think it will take me without pants."

"Just give us tonight to try, Granddad. If we don't get it tonight, I'll find your pants and you can go after it."

Panther James looked up at me suddenly. "Ah, the blond man," he said. "The pains I felt from the shovels in my stomach stopped tonight. Should I thank you for that?"

"No. Thank Hervey and that dog of his. I don't think they'll be back to bother your mound."

"That's good to hear," he said. "I'll be going there very soon and I would hate to end up in a museum."

"Come on, Granddad. You're too mean to die."

"Hah! That's what you think. I had a dream tonight. That's why I have to hurry. I want to get this thing about the land settled. We must get this settled, and little Eisa must mate with one of the Johnny Egret grandsons when she is of an age so that our people might go on for a while longer. . . ." His voice trailed off, and he looked at me again. His brown eyes had a milky tinge to them lanced with some inexorable understanding. "I'll trade you this fine watch for your pants," he said.

I smiled. "Maybe tomorrow, Mr. James."

"You just stay here, Granddad. We'll be right back. I've got something I need to prove to you."

We hustled back outside. Myrtle was waiting for us. Hervey still had the revolver he had taken from one of the mound robbers.

"Have you reloaded that shotgun?"

She nodded.

"Which way did that thing go?"

She pointed. "Just be careful, Hervey. I . . . really don't think that it's a man dressed up in a suit. The dogs always bark when strangers come. But when that thing is here, they just run. They run and hide. . . ."

We found the tracks by the creekbed at the edge of the clearing.

The mound robber had indicated that the track he had found was three feet long.

He was wrong. But not by much.

The tracks by the creek were the footprints of some gigantic barefooted man. Maybe twenty-five or thirty inches long. They were sunken deeply into the sand.

Hervey traced their outline with his flashlight. They were an awesome sight. I felt the strobing of body current move down my spine.

"Damn," whispered Hervey. "They're surefire deep enough."

"Look at your own tracks, though," I argued. "The sand's soft here. Your tracks are just as deep."

While Hervey held the light, I put my own foot in the swamp creature's track. And then I took a natural stride. It put me just short of the next track.

"If this thing's tall enough to touch the ceiling in Myrtle's house, he must have awful long arms—because his legs aren't any longer than mine. Plus, he was running. See the way the tracks sort of slide forward? He was running flat-footed."

The Chesapeake had found the tracks, too. He trotted between them, tail arched, nose testing the air.

"Go find! Gator! Go find!"

The dog took off on a run, and we followed behind.

He led us across the creek, through the edge of a cypress head, and then back to the road.

It was faster going on the road, and we fell farther and farther behind. Every now and then we'd stop to catch our breath and to check the trail. The huge footprints confirmed that the dog was on the right track.

We ran for about ten minutes before the Chesapeake started barking in the distance. It was an eerie sound, that rumbling *whuff* filtering through the swamp and the darkness.

"He's on to him," Hervey said excitedly. "He don't start barking until he can see what he's after!"

We increased our pace.

Hervey was right. The dog had caught up to the creature, all right.

As we got closer we could hear the savage growling. And we could hear someone yelling—a man yelling. His words were lost in the depths of the swamp, but it was clear that he was yelling for help.

And then we heard more voices.

And then a gunshot, followed by the wild yipping of the retriever.

Hervey stopped cold. "Oh no—they shot him. They shot my dog!"

He didn't have any trouble keeping up with me now. We sprinted along the dirt road, side by side. Suddenly the yipping stopped, followed by an ominous silence.

We came around a bend to see the red back-up lights of a car. There were dim shapes in the car, too dark to recognize. The car peeled around in the sand. The sweep of headlights gave us a panorama of cypress swamp: silver trees draped with moss, wild orchids in full bloom.

And something else.

The dark outline of a dog lay still in the middle of the road.

It was the Chesapeake.

At first I thought someone was shooting at us. I dropped belly first into the sand.

And then I realized that it was Hervey. He had been just behind me. He held the small-caliber revolver in both hands, firing all six rounds toward the car.

But at that distance, I knew there was little chance of any of the slugs finding the mark.

The car roared off, spewing sand and dust.

Hervey was silent for a long moment. "The bastards," he said softly. And he walked toward the fallen dog.

The Chesapeake rested side down in the sand as if asleep. Hervey kneeled and stroked the dog's head, then studied the blood on his hand.

"Shot him in the head," he said in a voice I had never heard before.

While it was true the dog and I had been anything but close, I had still admired him. And I found myself kneeling beside Hervey, hand stroking the dog's side.

And that's when I noticed something. "Hey—hey, Hervey! He's still breathing!"

"What? Damn!" Hervey put his ear down against the dog. "He is breathing. And his heart's just pounding away strong as ever."

I took the flashlight and studied the dog's wound. There was a line of bare flesh clear across the top of the dog's head. I fingered it gently.

"The bullet never went in. Must've just knocked him out or something."

And then there was something else I noticed. I pulled the dog's jaws open and removed a chunk of material. The material was coated with synthetic hair on one side and had a soft liner on the other.

The dog stirred when I removed it. He whined softly, then got shakily to his feet. When he saw Hervey, he managed to wag his tail a couple of times and give him a quick lick in the face. In a few more minutes he was walking and sniffing the ground again.

Hervey, the big stoic bear, was like a little kid with a

long-lost friend. He followed after him and actually cooed.

When he was finished with endearments, sure that the dog would be able to make it back to camp where we could treat his wound, I handed the material to Hervey.

"Here's our swamp monster," I said.

Hervey studied it with disgust, almost tossed it away, then thought better. "We'll show this to my granddad," he said. "And once we get him feeling better about what's really going on we'll hunt those bastards down. It shouldn't take long now that we know who they are."

"We do."

He looked at me oddly. "You mean you didn't recognize them?"

"Hell, I couldn't see their faces. It was too dark."

"The *car*," he said. "You didn't recognize the car? It was a big blue Cadillac. Had one hubcap missing from the left rear wheel. Remember those jerks back in Flamingo? It was the same car they drove away in!"

We took our time walking back to camp. Hervey kept a close check on Gator. Every time the dog stopped to lap swamp water, we stopped with him.

Hervey was in a better mood now, almost a party mood. We considered reasons why the boss man and his peons might want Panther James to abandon his Indian land. He seemed sure we would be able to stop them now. He even suggested that we contact a friend of mine at the Monroe County Sheriff's Department and get the law in to take care of them.

"I'm just afraid, Dusky, that if I got my hands on those bastards again," he explained, "that I wouldn't stop until they were dead. And I'm too handsome to spend the next forty years playing one-on-one with ratshit up in Raiford."

I laughed at that.

I was feeling better, too—but for one thing. I finally had to mention it to Hervey.

"Something about all this bothers me," I said.

He eyed me sharply. "Yeah?"

"I think you know what it is. The guy playing the part of the Swamp Ape—Myrtle's dogs never barked at him. She said they ran scared. But scared or not, they should have barked at a stranger."

He nodded. "I was thinking the same thing." He thought for a moment. "There are about twelve people in the Johnny Egret clan. Two families. They're close with Myrtle and all—but not so close that they visit every day. The dogs would know them, but not well enough not to bark."

"And that leaves Myrtle's husband."

"I hate to say it, but you're right. Billy Cougar. I only met him once. Came up for the wedding about seven years ago. He's never been able to hold a job. Like Myrtle says, he drinks heavy. But that still don't explain why he would turn against his own people."

I shrugged. "All we can do is watch him. From the looks of things, your dog got a piece of whoever it was in that gorilla costume. May have damaged him. If he comes back tonight with a dog bite, we're going to have to tell Myrtle."

"You mean I'm going to have to tell Myrtle," he said wryly.

So we were both feeling better—assured that there was some light at the end of the tunnel; some solution, however painful, to this thing which had been vexing Hervey's family.

I should have known then.

All the little alarms should have gone off.

Because it's one of life's sour tricks to make things seem easiest just when they are about to go from bad to worse.

MacMorgan's Law: When everything is coming up roses, get ready to order some bandages—because the roses always come with thorns.

So I should have guessed. But I didn't.

Instead, we made our way back to camp, chortling and joking and trading theories about why our businessmen adversaries had contrived such a bizarre plot.

Even Gator was walking better. And he even managed a snarl when one of the cur dogs came trotting up to greet us.

Hervey had the swath of costume hair in his hand. He was anxious to show his granddad. He was anxious to prove that the old man's dreams had been all wrong, and that they were going to keep the land, and their race would go on, and everyone was going to live happily ever after.

He went through the door into the chickee first.

At first, I couldn't understand why he stopped so suddenly.

I peered over his head and saw: Panther James had found his pants. He was stretched out on the dirt floor as if asleep. In the weak oil-lamp glow, the colors of his rag shirt blended into soft bands of blue and green and gold. He had knocked over the lone wooden chair when he fell. His old western hat had rolled across the floor.

There is something unmistakable about the look of death. The muscles slacken and the skin turns to paste. But more than that, the face—never so relaxed as in death—seems to return to the gentler contours of youth.

Panther James looked younger than before. The great hawk nose, the abrupt Indian cheeks, the firm chin were those of the long-gone youth who had hunted the swamps and fished the streams.

And even in death, he had the final proof of his wisdom: His dreams had not lied.

Mechanically, Hervey bent over his grandfather and

checked the pulse as if hoping for the same miraculous recovery his dog had made.

But it was useless.

"He's gone," he said simply.

"I'm sorry."

I expected tears, or at least moistening of eyes. But it did not come. "He was a fine man," Hervey said. "He taught me the woods. I used to wish I could be Indian, too. But it's more than just blood. . . ."

He looked down at the old vehicle which had once held Panther James. He sniffed once, wiped his nose. "I just decided we ain't going to call the law in on this, Dusky."

"I can see that."

"He died still believing that some swamp creature was going to take Eisa because he had somehow failed the land. He could have died in peace. Instead, they made it so he died with a lot of things unfinished; a lot of questions unanswered. I'm going to make them pay for that, Dusky. I feel like I've got to. Do you think that's silly?"

"If it's silly, you've got company," I said. "Tomorrow, while you take care of the funeral arrangements, I'll go to work. I'll start tracking them. . . ."

《 XIV 》

The afternoon after Panther James died, they buried him on the far edge of the mound near the ring of silver cypress trees which held the pond he had fished as a boy.

Myrtle James Cougar had accepted the news of her father's death more stoically than I had anticipated. But late that night, while Hervey slept, I heard her sobbing through the plank walls of the shack.

The next morning, red-eyed, she busied herself with contacting the women of the Johnny Egret clan, who would prepare the death feast while the Egret men went with Hervey and me to dig the grave and ready the mound.

There were three of them—a man who seemed a little younger than Panther James, and his two sons, who were both well into their forties. Upon first meeting them, I found myself looking for fresh cuts on arms or face—signs of dogbite.

But there was none.

They were a stoic threesome, but friendly enough. They found the way I beat the bushes looking for snakes quite funny.

It made me think of the way Panther James had laughed at my friend Grafton McKinney.

While Johnny Egret supervised, we filled in the trenches dug by the graverobbers and picked up all the beer cans and cigarette wrappers. After the old man had surveyed the site and agreed the job was finished, they set about finding a proper place to bury Panther James.

I stayed in the background and listened to them talk. Hervey and Johnny Egret finally settled on a shady place at the far edge of the mound near the cypress head. They agreed that when the graverobbers inevitably returned, they would probably start at the middle of the mound—as they all do.

You could tell it was an unpleasant subject to the older man. To him, the trenches and the litter were all symbols that he too would probably fall victim to the artifact hunter's shovel. Just as his sons would. And probably their children.

It was not easy work busting through the roots to softer ground where Panther James would be placed. And when we were halfway done, Hervey looked up at me and wiped his forehead with a sweaty hand.

"Some lemonade would be good, wouldn't it?" I said.

He looked perplexed. "Lemonade?"

I nodded. "You know—lemonade." The other men were listening, and I couldn't say what I really meant. Myrtle's husband hadn't returned home that night. And I didn't want him to get back and leave again before we had a chance to get a look at him. "Up at the house," I said. "Why don't you walk back there and get the lemonade?"

Suddenly understanding, he shook his head quickly. "Oh, the *lemonade*. Tell you what, Dusky, since this is family business, why don't you walk back and get it? You've worked harder than any three men. So take a break."

As I walked away, the Chesapeake thumped his tail at me. He rested in the shade with his bandaged head. He looked more ridiculous than fearsome.

"Watch out for snakes," one of Johnny Egret's son yelled over his shoulder.

They all laughed.

The women were in the yard preparing a long table with food. Even Myrtle wore traditional dress now: ankle-length skirts sewn of colorful cloth, shawls over their shoulders, layers and layers of beads that seemed to elongate their necks.

Only Eisa wore jeans and T-shirt. She played in the shade with two raven-haired boys about her own age. The boys were showing off for her, each trying to top the other. One did handstands. The other did somersaults. Eisa clapped her hands gleefully.

In the hands of those three children rested the future of this ancient and little-known band of Indians—the Tequesta.

Myrtle smiled when she saw me, and slipped away from the other women at my signal.

"You look like you've been working hard," she said. The change to traditional Indian dress complimented her. It brought out the earth colors of her skin and accented her crow-black hair.

"Not as hard as the others. I spent a lot of my time making sure I didn't get snakebit."

She chuckled. "I don't blame you."

There was an awkward pause while I scanned for a way to ask tactfully about her husband. She seemed to sense it. The smile left her handsome face.

"You're wondering what happened to the pickup truck?"

"I hadn't noticed that it was gone."

"You're a very bad liar, Dusky MacMorgan. All basically honest people are."

136

"Then I should be an expert."

"I think we both know better."

"Then maybe I should come right out and ask about your husband. Hervey told you about Gator tearing a chunk out of the Swamp Ape's costume. We're both wondering why the dogs didn't bark."

I could see that it was an unpleasant subject. She turned to look at the other women working. She nodded toward her little house.

"I think we should talk inside."

I nodded and followed her up to the house. She brought me a glass of cool well water, and we sat on the sparse furniture.

"He was here this morning?"

"Yes," she said. "He was here. I told him about Papa. He seemed anxious to leave when he heard." There was a resigned look of sadness in her face. "It is very hard for me to accept the possibility that he has something to do with all . . . this. But I think I suspected him all along. Maybe that is why I wanted so very much to believe there really was a swamp monster. My own husband . . ."

"But why? Why in the world would he go to such lengths? Wouldn't the property become his after your father's death anyway?"

She shook her head. "It's clan land—and he's a Cougar, remember. He's not really Tequesta at all. The land would become mine. Mine and Eisa's." Her voice broke, and she took a moment to get hold of herself. She said, "This next thing is very hard for me to say. You will be the first person I have told. We have not been a happy husband and wife," she said. "Our people blame it on Billy's drinking and gambling. But I know that I am just as much to blame."

I started to say something, but she cut me off. "No," she said. "Let me finish. If that was Billy in the swamp-creature costume, you would not expect a father to frighten his own child so badly."

"That's the main thing in his defense."

"Then he has no defense," she said flatly. "You see, Dusky, Eisa is not his child."

I said nothing, waiting for her to finish.

"Today you met Angus Egret, one of Johnny Egret's two sons. Angus has a fine wife. She is working outside now. Seven years ago I fell in love with Angus. And he was in love with me. In other times, he would have moved his things out of their chickee and would have come to live with me, because that was the old way—and we were very much in love. But ways have changed. Instead, he seeded me with child. But could not become my husband. He was already with a wife, you see?"

"Did Billy Cougar know?"

She shook her head. "Not at first. I knew that it was necessary that I marry quickly. Billy was available. I knew that he drank and that he gambled. I did not know that he would beat me—and beat my child," she added bitterly. "Like I said—it has not been a happy marriage."

"No one knew but you and Angus?"

"Papa knew. He told me one day after Eisa was born. He saw it in a dream. I expected him to be upset. He wasn't. He was very glad that Eisa was pure Tequesta. He liked Angus very much. Later, I think Billy began to suspect. There was nothing of him in Eisa. A parent would know. It made him that much meaner. We had no . . . relations after he began to suspect. He began to drink heavier. He spent all the money he made at the racetracks in Miami. In the last year or so, he's been acting even stranger. He keeps talking about moving. He never wanted to leave before. I think he has been on drugs. He is rarely home, and Eisa hardly ever sees him—and for that I am glad."

138

"What did he say when you saw him this morning, Myrtle?"

She shrugged. "Very little. His face was bandaged. He said that he had been in a fight. That's when I knew. Hervey had told me about his dog attacking the creature. Like I said, when he learned of Papa's death, he seemed very anxious to get away."

"Do you know where he went?"

"Not for sure. He has been working for a construction company near here."

"Do you know the name of it?"

She thought for a moment. "It's a new place. Like a sales station or something. It's called the Mickey Rather Development Corporation."

"Can you tell me how to get there?"

She could. He had about a half-hour head start on me. Rather than bother Hervey—and take the chance of his missing his grandfather's burial ceremony—I found the keys to the rental Ford and headed off alone through the cypress swamp toward the Tamiami Trail.

I felt bad for Myrtle James Cougar. Pick any race, any civilization, and the problems remain basically the same. People still struggle with the demands of the day-to-day—and a social structure in which love is too readily labeled as an infidelity.

Everything was beginning to add up.

Billy Cougar had always been a drinker and a gambler. And then he had fallen in with some construction company. You didn't have to be an Einstein to guess who ran the company. I pictured the four drunken businessmen in their safari suits at Flamingo.

Fate had given us an early shot at them. And we had blown it.

Now the scenerio demanded a final encounter; a last act. And I was more than ready.

In Florida—perhaps more than anyplace else—the

leisure-suit types carry too much weight. You get sick of their pushing and their wheeling-dealing and their own peculiar brand of development pornography.

People read their newspapers and worry out loud about the threat of destruction from nuclear-wielding countries. In truth, we face far more imminent danger from within. Steadily, inexorably, they sound our death knell with the roar of their dozers and their draglines, butchering our delicate land. They don't build. They embalm.

I held my breath while crossing the rickety bridge and turned left toward Naples. It was Sunday, and the traffic on the Tamiami Trail was heavier than before. Buggish Japanese cars and the shiny American gas hogs roared through the space and isolation of the 'glades, leaving cypress trees fluttering in their windwake.

I held the rental Ford on the narrow asphalt, trying to keep pace with the traffic. A Standard station that promised cold beer and cigarettes, a cluster of small houses, and a post office the size and shape of an outhouse heralded the little settlement of Ochopee.

I followed Myrtle's directions on past the Golden Lion Motor Inn—looking distinctly out of place in this wilderness of cypress and grass—and the Wooten Airboat ride concession with its red-white-and-blue streamers.

The dirt road I was looking for was just before the turnoff to Everglades City and the Seminole-style Highway Patrol station there.

A bright metal sign screamed at me:

Mickey Rather Construction/Sales
Building for a Better Florida

And don't they all?

I made the turn, worrying about the haze of dust the car trailed behind.

Myrtle had told me the construction office was about five miles inland. I decided to drive all but the last mile, then hide the car as best I could.

My plan was simple: just get a look at the layout so Hervey and I could return that night.

There was still the unanswered question: Why had Rather, the big boss man, gone to such bizarre lengths to make Panther James abandon his land?

If Hervey and I could break in that night and get a look at his records, we might be able to find out.

I kept a close eye on the car's odometer. After three miles, I slowed to an idle. The place was closer than Myrtle had guessed. Beyond the bend, above a crop of Australian pines, I could see a protruding television antenna.

I had passed a little clearing, so I stuck the car in reverse and backed up. The red car was easily seen behind the circle of oaks, but it couldn't be helped.

I wouldn't be long.

I made my way through the brush toward the antenna. Sandspurs grabbed at my pants, and mosquitoes whined in the shade of trees, away from the September heat.

The Mickey Rather construction and sales site was nothing more than a mobile home on cement blocks. It had a take-the-money-and-run look to it.

The trailer sat in the middle of a large shell drive. There was a mound of building material' under a tarp beside it, and a big yellow Bucyrus bulldozer. Beyond that, near the edge of a cypress head, sat two jeeps. One was new, the other World War II vintage. They both had big balloon wheels with chains belted to the tread.

In front of the mobile home was the dark-blue Cadillac. And the pickup truck I had seen at Panther James' camp.

I was about two hundred yards away, peering through the brush. Occasionally a dim shape would cross the curtained windows.

I was trying to decide whether to try and get a closer

look or just wait until I came back that night with Hervey when I heard the shot.

It was not the *crack* of a small-caliber weapon. It was the deep *thrump* of something big, like abbreviated thunder.

I ducked back into the bushes, wondering how in the hell they had seen me.

And then I realized they hadn't.

The door of the trailer swung open, and one of Mickey Rather's yes-men I recognized from Flamingo came running outside. There was a chunk of canvas covering the older jeep. He grabbed it and went running back into the mobile home.

I wasn't anxious to leave now. I was going to stay and see just what in the hell was going on.

After about five minutes, the door opened again. Rather's two yes-men were carrying something in the tarp. They had their jackets off and their ties loosened. They tried to hold the tarp away from their bodies as if it was distasteful—the way some people carry garbage.

Halfway to the jeep, one of them stumbled. The tarp buckled and a body came spilling out.

I had never seen Billy Cougar before, but there was little doubt that it was him. His face had been shot away, and the black Indian hair was matted with blood.

When they dropped him, Mickey Rather came charging out of the trailer. He looked this way and that anxiously, then yelled something at his two men. He held a long-barreled revolver in his hand. There was a chunk of gauze on his neck where the dog had gotten him.

So Billy Cougar had gone to report the news of Panther James' death to his new boss.

And something had gone wrong. Deathly wrong.

Billy Cougar had been a drunk and a gambler and had fallen in with the enemies of his people—and his land.

And he had paid the ultimate price for it. His life.

I watched them load the corpse into the newer of the jeeps, then cover the whole thing with a tarp.

Mickey Rather handed the revolver to one of his men, who trotted off toward the cypress head—probably to bury it.

And still the chunky boss man scanned the brush around the parking lot, as if looking for someone—or as if worried the law would come swooping down, sirens screaming, to catch them in the act.

I had seen enough.

Had the circumstances been different—had I been on an assignment—I would have begun planning a way to crack this construction ace and his men into a bunch of little pieces.

Instead, as I walked back to my car, I tried to think of ways to convince Hervey that this was now a matter for the law.

Until now, they hadn't really done anything illegal. A man can't kidnap his own daughter—even if he is dressed up in a gorilla suit.

And trying to scare people off their property—for whatever reasons—isn't right, but it's not the sort of thing that lasts long in court.

But now they had made the big jump. They had killed a man in cold blood.

And I was more than willing to be an eyewitness.

Mockingbirds chattered in the oaks above my car. I gave it a minute or two before stepping into the clearing.

In the process of loading the body and disposing the weapon, one of Rather's men had not made himself seen. And it was no time to take chances.

When I was sure no one was around, I walked quickly to the car, fired it up, and backed out onto the dirt road.

But that's as far as I got.

Because that's when I felt the cold steel of a revolver

pressed against the veeing where spinal cord enters the cranium.

The fourth man had hidden himself in my back seat.

"My, my, my, if it isn't Mr. Rough and Tough from Flamingo—no, don't turn around. I'll shoot you where you sit if you turn around. We're going to kill you anyway, but I'd like the boss to get a few cracks at you first. He was upset about the Flamingo episode, buster boy. Real upset. But your dying will make him feel a whole lot better. . . ."

≪ XV ≫

He made me drive around the bend to the mobile home.

He kept his left hand wrapped around my throat so I couldn't hit the accelerator, duck, and hope for the best.

Back in Flamingo, they had all looked doughy and overweight. But this guy knew how to handle a weapon—and a prisoner.

When we pulled up at the trailer, Mickey Rather's other two men jumped out from either side of the aluminum monstrosity. They both held revolvers. Obviously, they weren't expecting me. So this fourth guy's finding me had been a fluke. Or maybe just a reward for the boss man's vigilance. He had posted a guard—just in case.

The guy in the back seat kicked his door open and slowly climbed out. The revolver didn't waver for a moment. He was proud of his find—like a kid who's just found the prize Easter egg.

"Mickey—hey, Mickey! Look what I've got here. You remember this guy, don't you?"

He jerked me out of the car and shoved me back up against the fender. Mickey Rather came out of the trailer. He wore a white golf shirt that accented the size of his watermelon belly and his hammy biceps. A long black cigar was stuck in the middle of his mouth.

He didn't look any too happy.

He said to the guy who had caught me, "Anybody else with him, Benny?"

"No. No one. Just him, boss. I was keeping an eye on the road like you said. He parked his car a few hundred yards up. I got in the back and waited. The goddam mosquitoes about ate my butt off."

"Shut up, Benny." Mickey Rather had pale piggish blue eyes. He kept them pinned on me as he approached. He had a nervous mannerism—clenching and unclenching his fist. As before, he was slow. I saw the big roundhouse punch coming, and I had plenty of time to catch it in my own right hand. I squeezed just enough to let him know I could break his hand if I wanted, then shoved him away.

Mickey Rather didn't like being made a fool of in front of his men. His face turned crimson, and he clenched the cigar between his teeth.

"That was a stupid move, buster boy."

"I majored in stupid. But it saves on busted noses."

He looked at Benny. "If he so much as blinks an eye, shoot him."

"Glad to, boss."

So Mickey Rather got his next punch in. And his next. And his next. He was slow—but he hit like a sledgehammer. I had to fight to keep my feet.

"That's just to soften you up, buster boy." He was wheezing softly with effort. "Now, for openers, just who in the hell are you?"

"Just a good samaritan trying to help a friend."

His next punch caught me in the short ribs, knocking the wind out of me. "And I've had about enough of your smart-ass answers. I killed that goddam dog of yours last night, and we killed the Indian boy this morning. I'm not

146

in the waiting line for heaven, so you better not cross me again, buster boy. Now, who are you?"

I have found that in some tight situations the truth is often as good as a lie.

But not in this tight situation.

If I told him I was just some private snoop he would have had my carcass packed in the jeep alongside Billy Cougar's within the hour.

I had to give him something to think about; some reason to worry.

I gave it a few moments, as if struggling with my better judgment. I sighed and said finally, "You'll find out soon enough, Rather. So I guess there's no harm in telling you. I'm part of a federal investigative unit sent down here to check up on you."

He eyed me closely for a moment, trying to decide if I was telling the truth. I didn't doubt that he would. All crooks pay for their illegal profit with an unrelenting paranoia. They think everyone is after them.

"And just what put them onto an honest businessman like me?"

I shrugged. "What else? The IRS boys got suspicious. They've had their eye on you for a few years now."

He swore softly. "When I get my hands on that goddam bookkeeper . . ." His voice trailed off. All three of his men had their revolvers trained on me. He motioned with his head. "Tie him up, gag him, and lock him inside. I'm going to check out his story."

"You ain't going to let him go, are you, boss?" Benny seemed disappointed someone might steal his prize.

Mickey Rather sneered at me. "Let him go? Don't be silly, Benny. Tonight Billy the Indian is gonna have some company. I just want to do things nice and neat, see. When I'm sure things are square, you'll take buster boy here out to the swamp, put a bullet through that pretty blond head, and feed him to the alligators."

"Does that mean the scam ain't gonna work, boss?" asked one of the others.

Rather looked at him as if he were an idiot. "Sure, Louie. We're gonna stay right here while every fed in the world comes looking for us. No, you stupid bastard, the scam ain't gonna work. The Indian boy blew it for us. He could've been setting pretty, but instead he had to try getting tough. So now we head for the islands until this thing blows over." He looked at me meaningfully. "And they can't prove no murder if they can't find no corpses. Tonight this trailer is going to catch on fire. And we're going to disappear in the smoke. . . ."

They were no Boy Scouts—so they did a more than thorough job of tying and gagging me. I'd much rather be tied by a knot expert than someone who doesn't know what he's doing. You can't back bad knots—they have to be cut.

So they used about twenty feet of tough hemp rope to bind arms, hands, and legs, taped my mouth, and rolled me into a narrow broom closet.

All I could do was lie there on my belly in a reverse fetal position and hope that Hervey would contact the law when I didn't return rather than come looking by himself.

But I knew better.

April had said it best: "He isn't the type to go whining to the law. . . ."

So he would come by himself. And they would be ready. And that would make three corpses to carry into the swamp that night.

I felt the nausea well up in my stomach. I could see again the crimson hole which had been the remains of Billy Cougar's face.

That was the way Hervey would look if I didn't think of something. And think of something fast. Hervey was one of the rare good ones. He had a wife and a beautiful daughter. He would be missed.

I spent the first hour trying to expand the rope; trying to wiggle free. I just about had my hands loose once—but then the door swung open and Benny stuck his ferret face inside.

He leered at me. "Damn if the boss wasn't right. He said check up on you 'cause you were the type to chew your own arm off if it took that to get away."

So he kicked me a couple of times in the stomach, then added more rope to arms and legs.

Escape was useless—for now, anyway.

So I resigned myself to the situation. My only chance would come that night when they carted me off to the swamp to kill me.

For some reason, dying in a swamp bothered me. I've always wanted to die at sea; just sort of go down and never come back up.

I remembered Panther James and his prediction that I didn't have long to live.

So maybe it would be the swamp after all. . . .

Mickey Rather had gone off for a while to "check out" my story—or so he had said. The walls of the mobile home were beer-can-thin, and when he returned I could hear them talking over the generator hum of the air conditioning.

He said that he had called one of his associates in Washington. They had heard nothing of an investigation. Rather said it didn't matter if I was telling the truth or not. He said the Indian had blown it.

Listening, I began to put it all together. Rather and his boys had operated an illegal gambling ring in Miami and built condominiums with the profit. They were speculators. He would find a choice bit of land, contract out the work, use the cheapest materials available, and then clip the retirees, selling his condominium apartments at extravagant prices.

Billy Cougar had gotten in deep to Mickey Rather at the card table and the racetrack. Rather had somehow learned about the unique land on which Cougar lived—probably from Billy Cougar himself. So Rather had taken Billy's IOUs until the Indian had no choice but to go along with Rather's plan.

I should have put it all together after talking to Graff McKinney. He was the one who had told me why the big-time gamblers were interested in Indian land. There would be no state control. And very little federal control.

For Mickey Rather, taking reign of the Panther James acreage would have been akin to finding the Holy Grail. It was a big-time gambler's dream come true. The plans for the casino he wanted to build there had already been drawn up. He would bulldoze a road through the swamps and add a ritzy hotel and, maybe in the future, add a condominium development.

By the time his opponents got things worked out in court, he would have already made his millions.

Billy Cougar had no choice but to go along with it. Besides, from what I had heard, he liked the idea of being rich anyway.

The only thing that stood in the way was the old man, Panther James. So Billy Cougar had concocted the idea of scaring him off through the materialization of some old Indian legend—the Swamp Ape.

But something had gone wrong. The old man had died. And Billy Cougar, suddenly realizing that he held all the cards, had gotten nasty. He had demanded more of the action. And he had tried to get tough when Rather refused.

So they had blown his face away. And now he rested beneath the tarp in the jeep—right along with Rather's dreams.

But I had to give credit to Mickey Rather. He wasn't one to linger on recent failures. He was already changing gears, planning a new future.

Through the walls, I could hear them talking.

"You don't think they'll send people looking for us, boss?"

"Hell yes, they will. But a man can buy a whole lot of privacy in South America. I've got the cash we were going to use for this project in a Cayman bank. We'll clean out the account, head for Argentina, and lay low for a while. Besides, I've got some connections there. We'll invest in the dope crops, and feed the profits into one of our subsidiary development corporations back here in Florida. As long as the land holds out, there's still plenty of dough to be made."

Slowly, surely, Mickey Rather broke down their reluctance to leave the country. He painted a picture of South Seas bliss for them. His men would have tropical drinks in the morning and beautiful island girls at night.

And the tone of his voice implied the alternative—death if they didn't follow him.

In the silences I knew they were pouring themselves more courage, drinking to their new future.

I kept hoping they would go into detail about how they would make their escape.

But they never did.

So I lay waiting in the squashed confines of the closet. My legs gradually went numb, and then my arms. I did flexing exercises trying to stay ready. I searched myself for fear of my impending death—and found none. When you have lost everything, there is no fear of that final forfeiture. There was only deep disquiet within me that demanded I try to find a way of going on; some life force that refused to give up as long as there were still good fish to catch, cold beer to drink, and long autumn days to enjoy.

Every hour or so, Benny would come to check on me, tighten the ropes, and add a few kicks. The kicks were for his boss, he would sneer. He had an ugly chuckle. He said that his boss was going to have to have plastic surgery because of my dog. And he wanted me to suffer for it.

It was what you would call one very long afternoon.

They came for me at first dark. Just as they had promised. Benny cut the ropes around my legs, and two of them jerked me to my feet. The muscles were so numb I could barely stand alone.

The hilarity was gone from them. They seemed nervous; anxious to be done with me and get the hell away.

Mickey Rather directed everything. His face looked bloated from drinking. The dogbite on his neck had begun to leak blood through the white gauze. He had them shove me outside. With my hands still bound, I landed face first in the sand.

"Watch he doesn't try and make a run for it," Rather warned.

"Hell, boss, he can hardly stand up, let alone run."

"Just don't take any chances—that's all I'm telling you. Louie, you stay here. Start spreading the gasoline. And don't screw up. When we torch this place I want everything to burn."

They dragged me to my feet. My brain kept scanning for some clever means of escape—but found none. I couldn't make a deal with them. Mickey Rather had too many options to be interested in a deal.

So I tried to make a run for it. I butted Benny in the stomach with my head, caught Rather between the legs with a well-placed kick, and took off in a numb dash.

But Louie dragged me down from behind, clubbing at my head with the grip of his pistol.

Rather rolled on the ground in pain. His face was pale—as if he was about to vomit.

He looked at Benny. "Get the jeep started!" he hissed.

Purposefully, he got to his feet. He turned a dead eye on me and said, "Kill him, Louie. Right through the head. I'm going to enjoy this. Buster boy, hold that breath you're taking—because it's going to be your last."

And just before I heard the explosion, as the double-action hammer *click-clicked*, I knew that he was right. . . .

《 XVI 》

I felt blood splatter hot across my face, and I rolled to the ground wondering why I felt no pain, thinking, strangely: If this is death, it's not so bad after all. . . .

There was another explosion, and someone collapsed beside me. Even with part of his head gone, the sneer was still affixed to Benny's face.

It wasn't until I heard the low roar of the Chesapeake that I knew for sure. The dog came out of the darkness and across the shell drive in about four long strides and knocked the fourth man backward. He had been drenching the trailer in gas. With Benny and Louie dead, Mickey Rather sprinted toward the idling jeep with its big balloon wheels. He had been smoking a cigar. He tossed it behind him, and the whole place went up with a *pewsh*.

I didn't see the fourth man run into the fire. But I heard his scream. I was too busy trying to roll away from the sudden searing heat of it.

Rather punched the jeep into gear and roared away toward the cypress head. The dog bounded after him, but there was a shrill whistle and he stopped in his tracks.

Hervey came charging out of the brush. He looked like

a creature from hell in the blazing light of the fire. The sawed-off twelve-gauge was still smoking. He knelt beside me and cut the ropes.

"Are you okay?"

"Bruised. And thankful. Very thankful. Thanks for showing up."

"Didn't have anything better to do," he said laconically.

I got to my feet, trying to work the muscles back to life.

"Let's get that other jeep started," I said.

"No way. From the way your head looks, you need a doctor. Now."

"Fine," I said. "Get a doctor. Bring two of them. I'll be back after I take a chunk or two out of Mickey Rather."

Hervey grinned. "Okay, okay—you drive. I'll reload."

The swamp buggy he had left us was no speed wagon. And we never got close enough to get a shot. It pounded and creaked dutifully through the swamp and over the high ground at a screaming fifteen miles an hour.

But it was easy enough to stay on Rather's track. His big four-wheel-drive left a snaking line of seeping ruts in the marsh, visible in the beam of our headlights.

"This thing won't go any faster?"

"For the fifth time—no."

"If he gets out on a road we've lost him."

"The last place he wants to be is on a road. And if he keeps on heading south we've got him. The 'glades doesn't go on forever."

A full moon, snow-bright, lifted in the east, and the marsh broke into plains of sawgrass, vast and golden like wheat. For the first time, we got a brief look at Mickey Rather. His jeep was a red speck of tail lights in the distance, at least two miles ahead of us.

Above him, stars glimmered like icy scars against the sky. Panther James would have seen them as omens. . . .

We drove on and on for another hour . . . maybe two. Small Everglades deer flushed before our headlights. And once we saw a hulk of a black bear amble across a flag pond and glare back at us. Behind us, the Chesapeake growled—but kept his seat.

Twice we almost got stuck and had to leave Rather's trail for higher ground. But each time we circled back on it. The ground kept getting marshier, breaking into sporadic islands of buttonwood and black mangrove. A gathering of laughing gulls in the moonlight told me we were getting near the Gulf.

"It's no use, Dusky. There's an old charcoal maker's road down here—Pahayokee Cross. He'll find it and be long gone by the time we get there."

"No way, Hervey. No way. You haven't noticed?"

He looked at me, perplexed. "Noticed what?"

"He's heading *west* all of a sudden. I don't know why. Maybe it's just temporary. But if he keeps on going he's going to run out of land real quick."

Hervey looked quickly around, trying to get his bearings.

"Damn," he said, "you're right."

"Mickey Rather may be a slick man in a business deal. But the only thing he knows about the wilderness is how to bulldoze it. I think our boy is lost. Lost and desperate—and that makes him dangerous."

"I'm not in a particularly good mood myself," said Hervey through tight lips.

He had told me about Panther James' funeral. And about how he had skipped out on the feast after Myrtle had told him where I had gone.

"Figured if you weren't back by dinnertime, you needed help bad. I know how much you hate to miss a meal."

Hervey had played it a little more cautiously than I had. He had parked his borrowed car just off the Tamiami Trail and walked the whole way to the mobile home through the back country. He had seen my car and reasoned that I was either inside or dead. So he had waited in the bushes, hoping they would make a move.

"I figured if you was still alive, I'd just hold them at gunpoint and take them to the law. But they sort of forced my hand when they decided to shoot you right then and there."

I told Hervey about Billy Cougar and the whole gambling scenario which had brought us to be winding our way through the Everglades in the moonlight.

"The bastards," he muttered when I had finished. "I never much liked Billy, but I'm sorry he got tied up with creeps like that. They're the kind who are ruining this state. Selfish. Selfish and money-hungry and stupid. They'll stop at nothing. And they won't be satisfied until it's all gone."

The moon was higher now; so bright you could see the pale outline of trees and the shadows of sloughs without the headlights.

Bullfrogs rumbled, and nocturnal birds squawked, and once, above the whine of the jeep, we heard the haunting scream of a Florida panther. There was a terrifying force in the noise, and had I not known what it was, I would have guessed that somewhere in the depths of the swamps, some woman had gone mad.

We came around a mangrove thicket to find the unexpected: Mickey Rather's jeep caught fender-deep in a tidal creek. Billy Cougar's body was still beneath the tarp in the back. Hervey and I jumped out, followed by the dog. Hervey held the shotgun at ready, thinking it might be a trap.

But it wasn't.

Through the steaming beams of the jeep lights we could see his tracks, two inches deep in the muck, trail off down the creekbed.

"After him on foot now?" I asked.

Hervey shook his head. "I'll back our jeep up and try to find a way through these mangroves. We'll let Gator track him from here."

The dog didn't need to be told. He was already casting back and forth in Rather's tracks.

In four-wheel drive, we idled on through the moonlight. A grassy slough paralleled the creek. We could hear the Chesapeake crashing through the water, searching.

Mickey Rather wasn't far away now. We saw him once in the sweep of our headlights. He looked back over his shoulder, the desperation strange and gray on his face. The gauze on his neck had come undone, and it fluttered by the ends of the tape. When he saw the dog coming after him, he took off at a heavy run. He stumbled once, fell, and pulled himself to his feet, already running again.

Then, suddenly, he just disappeared.

It didn't take us long to find out how. The slough ended abruptly at a black swath of water. It took us both a moment to get our bearings. We jumped out of the jeep, trying to make the water and islands and the vast moonlit desert of open Gulf make sense.

We looked at each other and said at the same time, *"The Shark River. . . ."*

Mickey Rather was a better swimmer than I would have guessed. We could see him clearly in the tunneling jeep lights. The Chesapeake dove in headlong after him, but Hervey whistled him back abruptly.

"I ain't sending him in there," Hervey said firmly.

And suddenly I knew what he meant.

"If Rather makes it across, he'll work his way to the beach on Cape Sable. He might be able to hijack a boat there."

"I don't care. I about lost that dog once. I ain't gonna take the chance again."

"Then I'll go."

I turned my back on Hervey's objections, kicking off my shoes. Mickey Rather was about halfway across. He was a fair swimmer, but he was no SEAL, and I knew I could catch him before he made it to the island on the other side. I ran into the water until it was waist-deep, then dove after him, swimming with head up, watching the dim shape in the distance.

About fifty yards out I saw it. I had thought it was the sort of thing you see once in a lifetime and never see again.

But I was wrong.

At first I thought it was just a fallen tree drifting in the moonlight.

But trees don't drift *up*current.

I stopped in the water, sculling, hypnotized by the size of the thing.

It was midway between Mickey Rather and me. I reached for the Randall knife on my belt and realized I hadn't worn it—and if I had, Rather's men would have taken it.

I should have sprinted back toward Hervey. But I couldn't. I was mesmerized—and it may have saved my life. Rather still splashed noisily across the river. The creature seemed to pause between us, as if deciding.

Then, suddenly, it submerged. I felt my breath coming soft and shallow, wondering if it was swimming along the bottom toward me—knowing that it was too late now to try to escape, because even I couldn't outswim such a magnificent thing.

There was a long minute of silence. Hervey was calling something behind me, but the words came to me in a jumble. They made no sense. Suddenly, Panther James' dream popped into my mind: *"You were in the water fighting a creature with many teeth. You thought it was a shark. But it wasn't a shark. . . ."*

159

So maybe this was another of his dreams coming to pass. . . .

But sometimes an old man's dreams aren't to be trusted, or maybe blind luck can alter a prescribed fate, or maybe nature just has its own sense of inevitable justice, because the giant saltwater crocodile didn't choose me that night.

Suddenly, through the silence, came a wild explosion from the water beyond me. The jeep lights showed a frothing geyser followed by a terrible scream. It was almost like a woman's scream—or the scream of a Florida panther.

The croc came halfway out of the water with Mickey Rather looking strangely small between its jaws. There was a look of confusion on his face, like that of a small boy. The bandage had been knocked from his neck, and he held his arms outstretched, as if bracing himself for a fall.

The croc took him back into the water, rolling him around and around. All you could see was the croc's tree-trunk tail and the rag-doll figure of Mickey Rather through the black froth.

And then there was silence.

A dark and total silence that echoed in the ears.

"Dusky—dammit, Dusky, get the hell out of there! Now!"

It was like waking up. I shook myself and headed back for shore in a long strong crawl. Hervey was there to pull me up on the bank. The dog trotted nervously beside him as if he, too, had realized for the first time that there are things on this earth for which no other creature is a match.

"You stupid bastard, why did you stay in there so long?"

Hervey had been scared—and the fear had made him mad.

I spit brackish water, touching the bruises on side and stomach from the beatings I had taken.

"It had Rather. He was food enough. I had no reason to worry."

"Yeah? Then there must be two of them."

He swung me around and pointed. There, where I had crawled up the bank, was the croc. His head was the size of a tapered coffee table. A chunk of Mickey Rather's pants protruded from the jumble of teeth. His eyes glowed in the jeep lights, blood-red and menacing, challenged but undefeated. . . .

« XVII »

On a September afternoon filled with saffron light and the smell of jasmine, I rode my ratty ten-speed bike through old Key West, then along Roosevelt Boulevard, and turned right down the dirt road to Yarbrough's Marina and Boat Service.

He had stayed on in the Everglades for a few days to comfort Myrtle and to talk to the law-enforcement boys. He had insisted that I have nothing to do with it; assured me that it would be a simple matter of answering questions and explaining just why there were four new corpses in south Florida and one man who had disappeared completely.

He was right—or so he told me over the phone from Monroe Station.

My blind lie to Mickey Rather that the feds were after him had hit the mark. They were—but we had beaten them to the punch.

So they called it self-defense and buried them and their files away. Myrtle, said Hervey, had at first been shocked by Billy Cougar's murder, but then just relieved. She finally reasoned that he would have drunk himself to death anyway, and besides, it was time that Eisa had a proper father. And when the right man came along, she said, she would know. Until then, Johnny Egret's third unmarried son had returned from Immokalee to comfort her. . . .

So I hadn't seen Hervey since he'd returned. And I hadn't even bothered to call April—for reasons I couldn't verbalize. I just knew it had something to do with her youth in conflict with my own lethal life-style.

Whatever the reasons, I knew that she wouldn't be any too happy with me.

I leaned my bike against one of the draping oaks in the yard by the board house. Chickens scratched and bickered in the sand, and the Chesapeake thumped his tail lazily at me from the shade and lifted his head, showing the bare racing-stripe scar between his eyes. He got to his feet, gave me two grudging licks, on the hand, then collapsed in the shade.

Hervey met me at the door. His wife, small and squat with her Indian good looks, smiled at me from the kitchen. But there was a nervousness to the smile—and then I noticed the nervousness in Hervey.

"Dusky . . . hey—good to . . . ah . . . see you!"

I looked at him strangely. "What's wrong with you, Yarbrough? You look as if I just caught you stealing something."

"Stealing—hah! That's a good one, Dusky. Why don't you and me jump into the boat and head on out to the reefs? Grab us a few lobster for dinner, what say? I got a spot out there none of them sporty divers know about—"

He didn't have time to finish.

And suddenly I knew why Hervey and his wife were so nervous.

April came walking down the hall from her bedroom. I had never seen her so beautiful—or wearing a dress, for that matter. It was one of those prim cotton print things with a knee-length skirt that accented her figure and the black sheen of her hair. Her long legs seemed to glow within the stockings, and her perfect face held an odd pixyish smile.

"Why, Dusky! I have someone here I'd like you to meet."

She trailed the man along behind her, holding his hand. He was a frail, bookish-looking guy about my age. He wore a tweed jacket over an open sports shirt, and he had that maddening aloofness of the self-styled intellectual.

"Dusky, this is a friend of mine from the university, Professor Noel Watson. He'll be staying with me for awhile. He's doing research. Noel—this is Dusky. He's an old friend of the family."

We shook hands. First meetings can tell you much. He didn't like me. I didn't like him. I sat in the living room for as long as I could stand it, making small talk. At first, April seemed to enjoy the confrontation. But then I could see that it was hurting her, too, so I made my excuses and escaped outside, sucking in the fresh September air like an animal just out of captivity.

All the way back to the marina at Garrison Bight I swore at myself, called myself improbable names, suggested that I perform impossible acts upon my own person.

"Sometimes you're just too goddam stupid for words!" I told myself.

"Absolutely!" I agreed.

The phone booth in the marina parking lot gave me a flash of inspiration. The operator gave me the number of the Flamingo bar and restaurant. A woman with a smoker's voice answered. Could she connect me with Stella Catharine Cross' apartment?

She could and did.

Stella seemed happy to hear from me. At first. But then that same strange nervousness came into her voice.

"Dusky, I'd really love to go cruising with you, but . . ."

164

In the background, I heard a man's voice. He wanted to know who she was talking to.

I thanked her for the long-gone evening, agreed to her demands that I call again, and hung up.

So what do the lonely ones do in Key West?

They make the rounds of the bars, get drunk, and hunt for meteoric crossing of lust, willingness, and mutual boredom.

But I just wasn't up for that.

So I rode my bike dejectedly across the parking lot to the dock where *Sniper* was moored. Bored with swearing at myself, I whistled an aimless tune.

"Hey—hey, Dusky!"

I looked up to see Steve Wise, dockmaster and Key West playboy. He had his hands stuffed in his pockets and an unusually forlorn look on his face.

He shrugged at me. "You look like you just lost your best friend," he said.

"Does that bear any resemblance to a jilted lover?"

He actually smiled. "You too, huh?"

"Me too?"

He nodded over his shoulder. Behind him, aboard his chunky houseboat, the two Playmate twins seemed to be having a discussion. Or an argument. They wore thin bikinis that grabbed at the heart. Their chins were speared out at each other, their faces red. Suddenly, one of them held up a fierce middle finger—an unmistakable gesture. And, just as suddenly, the other grabbed a beach sandal and hurled it at her.

Steve sighed dejectedly. "No matter what those Mormons say, one man can't please two women. Not at the same time, anyway."

"And sometimes you can't please even one."

"God, I'm sick of them."

"I know the feeling."

"Women! To hell with them." He eyed my boat, a new

look on his face. "Dusky, do you realize I haven't booked you for a charter all week?"

I was beginning to catch on. "Is that right?"

"Dusky, how far do you think we could cruise in a week?"

"How long will your twins be staying on your house-boat?"

"Five more long days. I can't take it. God, I can't get any sleep and I'm losing weight."

"Then I think the two of us could make the Tortugas in a day—then take four days getting back."

He smiled, suddenly happy. "I'll get the beer."

"I've got plenty."

He hesitated. "Any women out there in the Tortugas?"

"Occasionally."

"What the hell," said Steve Wise. "I'll take the chance. . . ."

*Here's an exciting glimpse of the
thrilling adventure that awaits you
in the next novel of this action-
packed series:*

MacMorgan #7:
GRAND CAYMAN SLAM

The corpse was gone, but the sprawled outline was still there, traced in white chalk.

The floor was of pale wood. Not pine, but some kind of tropical planking that held the metallic stink of blood—a black amoeba splotch that had rivered beyond the chalk confines and dried.

"You found her just like this?"

"Aye. I did, mate."

"And they think you murdered her?"

"They *thought* I'd murdered her. Can you imagine—a sweet lad from the home soil like meself?"

I turned away from the outline on the floor. The cop who had traced the corpse had caught the feminine curvature of hips and the delicate fingers of the left hand, thrown out wildly to stop her fall.

Only there was no stopping that fall. It was the final descent.

Death.

There was something grotesque about a thing so temporary as chalk marking the resting spot of a being who had lived and laughed and loved, only to rendezvous, face down, with wood and a knife slit across the throat.

That plus the stink made me feel unexpectedly queasy. Unexpected because I've seen plenty of death before. But there was a coldness to this white outline of a woman that I would never know. Like so many things the cops do, it seemed to reduce murder to a faceless shape, complete with bloodstain.

"Mind if we step out onto the porch?"

"Aye. I canna stand the sight of the blinkin' thing meself."

I followed him outside. The screen door slammed behind us. Beyond the black growth of gumbo limbo, mahogany, and jasmine, stars threw paths upon the Caribbean sea. It was one of those soft winter nights in the tropics. The sort of night people come to Grand Cayman to enjoy. The wind was cloying, blowing off the sea, and you could hear the roar of waves upon the reef, half a mile out.

"You knew her, right?"

The features of my good friend, Wes O'Davis, seemed softer by the yellow porch light. Or maybe by the finding of a dead woman upon his living room floor. There was the broad, Gaelic face and the Viking beard and the ugly broken nose—but the pale eyes seemed withdrawn, as if he were someplace else.

"Did I know tha' poor wee girl? Aye, I knew her. Treated 'er like a tramp, I did."

"Is this a confession?"

"Hah! Might as well be, lad. Might as well be." He stepped off the porch and kicked at a big conch shell—forgetting he was barefoot, apparently. He jumped around for a second, then grabbed the shell and gave it a savage toss. You could hear it hit the water. "I treated her like a brute, I did," he said.

"But you didn't kill her?"

" 'N do I look like a murderer to you, Mr. Dusky MacMorgan?"

"You *look* like you are capable of robbing churches and assaulting nuns."

"I take it that's a 'yes'."

"It is."

"So you think I killed her?"

"I didn't say that. I know you, remember? I know you're no murderer. But you called me down here to help, right? So let me help. Shake off that case of the guilts you have at least long enough to tell me what in hell happened. Ever since I got here you've been tight as a drum. A blacksmith couldn't get a pin up your ass with a hammer. Just relax—I'm a friend, remember?"

He rolled his shoulders, flexing his neck. Then he gave the sudden leprechaun grin that I knew so well. "Yer right. I'll be needin' to fill you in on all the particulars—if yer ta help me, that is."

"Okay, good. So talk. You knew the girl."

"Aye. Monster that I am, I knew her the way I've known a hundred other lonely tourist ladies. They come to Grand Cayman by themselves, or with a husband who is no longer very attentive."

"Then you step in."

He nodded. "In me own defense, Yank, I must say most a them seem the happier for it."

"What was her name?"

"Cynthia. Cynthia Rothchild. Met 'er at one of those snooty little teas in Georgetown. We're still very English here in the Caymans, ye know."

"She was wealthy?"

"Said she was a nanny. Had the care of a boy child fer some very rich folks from London. Sir Conan James and Lady James. Sir James has an advisory position with Government House, appointed by Her Majesty. That's why I was invited to the snooty tea."

"As a bodyguard?"

He shrugged. " 'Tis probably the real reason. But they said me attendance was required so they could present me with some damnable award."

I smiled. "From the queen?"

"Aye. Pretty little thing it is, too. Lady James pinned it on. A great beauty, that Lady James. Magnificent woman —even if she is English."

"But you settled for the nanny, Cynthia Rothchild."

"Aye. She was something of a beauty herself, Yank. Very black hair. Lovely figure. You know me weakness fer the ladies. Saw her three—no, four times. She'd drive her wee rental car over from Three Mile Beach when the lad was asleep."

"And spend the night?"

"Aye. The best part of it."

"So she lived on the island."

"Sir James keeps a home here. But they live in London."

"And he didn't mind his nanny sneaking out?"

"He's a bit of a womanizer himself, I'm afraid. So I'm sure he understood. Besides, Her Majesty honored me with an award, remember? Sir James would overlook such a thing with me."

"When's the last time you saw her?"

"In the afternoon, day before yesterday. We had lunch together. She seemed very nervous, Yank. Bothered me, did. She had the lad with 'er—little Tommy. Fine-looking boy, 'bout twelve. Something of a genius, to hear Lady James talk. A regular wizard. That night I supped at Betty Bay Point, made the rounds of the pubs with a few of me island mates, and then went home. She was layin' on the floor of me living room. Part a 'er dress was ripped away. She had this awful look a surprise on 'er face. Her throat had been cut."

"And you called the police?"

"Aye. Rang up the substation at Bodden Town. The constable is a friend a mine. He seemed very sorry to have to arrest me. That's when I called you."

"I was kind of surprised you met me at the airport."

"They knew straight away I didn't do it. I was with me mates, remember? Besides, Sir James found the note."

"What note?"

The Irishman picked up another conch shell and threw it in a moonlit spiral toward the Cayman sea. "The ransom note, Yank. They've taken little Tommy. Kidnapped 'im, they did. Sir James has seventy-two hours to pay them two million pounds. So that gives us three days to find the kidnappers, snatch the lad, and bring him safely home."

"Wait a minute—does Sir James want you to get involved?"

"Her Majesty does, Yank. It's a dangerous precedent to set—a true Irishman serving the Queen. But they killed me little Cynthia. And she was a fine, sweet girl with a pretty laugh and a wonderful way beneath the covers. She was too good for the likes of me, Yank. Treated 'er like nothin' but a sleepover. So now it's me duty to make amends. And yer jest mean enough to help. Three days, Yank—that's all we have. An' three days is all those bloody buggers have to live. . . ."

ABOUT THE AUTHOR

Randy Striker is a charterboat captain out of Fort Myers, Florida who writes novels in his spare time.